"Just try to lasso me."

Looking at Travis, standing so arrogantly, with his legs braced apart and his black Stetson low over his brow, Rachel wanted nothing more than to put him in his place. "My pleasure, cowboy," she drawled.

"Like to play rough?" he taunted as she swung the rope. "So do I." He caught it and reeled her in with a fast hard yank, but he knew immediately there was nothing rough about the soft way their legs and stomachs were aligned now. "It can get very hot here in the summer," he managed to warn softly. "Too hot for some."

"Then you better head for the air-conditioning, Travis," Rachel countered. "'Cause I love the heat."

His eyes darkened. His head lowered. His lips parted. "I love the heat, too, sugar." His voice vibrated with passion and his eyes sparkled with mischief. "So you better watch out."

Dear Reader,

No doubt you've noticed the different look to your American Romance novels. Now you're about to discover what's new between the covers.

Come with us and sail the high seas with a swashbuckling modern-day pirate...ride off into the sunset on the back of a motorcycle with a dark and dangerous man...lasso a cowboy Casanova and brand him your own. You can do it all with the *new* American Romance!

In this book, and every book each month, you'll fall in love with our bold American heroes, the sexiest men in the world, as they take you on adventures that make their dreams—and yours—come true.

Enjoy the new American Romance—because love has never been so exciting!

Sincerely,

Debra Matteucci
Senior Editor & Editorial Coordinator
Harlequin Books
300 East 42nd St., 6th floor
New York, NY 10017

CATHY GILLEN THACKER

THE COWBOY'S MISTRESS

Harlequin Books

TORONTO • NEW YORK • LONDON
AMSTERDAM • PARIS • SYDNEY • HAMBURG
STOCKHOLM • ATHENS • TOKYO • MILAN
MADRID • WARSAW • BUDAPEST • AUCKLAND

Beth—

This one's for you, sis.
When you read it, you'll know why.

Published September 1992

ISBN 0-373-16456-4

THE COWBOY'S MISTRESS

Chapter One

"It's six o'clock. Do you know where your children are?"

Rachel Westcott looked up at the sound of the low masculine voice, and Travis Westcott had the satisfaction of watching his former sister-in-law's face pale with the shock of seeing him again after nearly seventeen years.

When her shock faded, he saw her confusion. Was it true? Did she have no clue as to what the twins were up to, as they had claimed? Well, there was one way to find out. Travis sauntered into her spacious office at the Tradewinds Travel Agency and shut the door behind him.

"Well, do you?" he provoked lazily. He wished she weren't so damn beautiful and that he wasn't so distracted by her incredibly good looks.

"Of course I know." Her chin lifted a haughty notch and she fastened her wide golden-brown eyes on his. "They're at home."

"Guess again," he said tightly, aware that though she was just a year younger than him, which made her thirty-four, she had the poise of an older woman and the stunningly perfect physique of a younger one. More disturbing than that was his discovery that she still had what she'd always had, even at the tender age of seventeen—an elusive striking quality that always caused a man to look twice. Rachel couldn't go anywhere without heads turning. Some called it charisma. Some called it magic.

Rachel was silent. He could see the pulse beating in her throat, but she held whatever she was feeling about him at that moment firmly in check. "No, I don't think I will guess," she said.

Because he knew it would irritate her, he let his gaze drift over her fair translucent skin and wildly curling shoulder-length flame-red hair. "I think you'd better."

Her soft bow-shaped lips tightened into an irritated pout. "I don't want to play games with you, Travis."

"Believe me, this isn't fun for me, either."

She viewed him with utter condescension. "You've obviously come here to tell me something, so why don't you get on with it?"

Travis saw no reason to make it easy for her. "I thought you might want to explain yourself first," he drawled as he took a seat on the corner of her desk and cocked his head to one side. "Or perhaps I should say, explain your children."

Keeping the bulk of the desk between them like a protective shield, she drew herself up to her full five foot five. "How do you even know I *have* children?"

Travis shrugged, watching her toss her hair out of her face. He wished he could think of another way, besides kissing her, to quickly extinguish the cool challenge in her eyes. "I don't really. At this point, I'm just going on what the twins claim."

At the mention of the word twins, her face turned very white. She gripped the edge of her desk with both hands.

"They're at the ranch now," Travis continued, taking some satisfaction in the way she was beginning to shake. "With my mother."

Rachel sat down because she knew if she didn't she was going to fall down. "What do you mean the twins are at the ranch?" she repeated in a low tight voice.

"Just what I said," Travis returned impatiently, looking older and more savvy now, but no kinder. He was no less the quintessential Texas bad boy than he had been years before. "They're there."

"At the ranch?" she repeated shakily, taking in his ruggedly carved face and slate-blue eyes. "That's impossible. They don't even know... I never told them."

Travis lifted a thick black brow. His mouth curved cynically. "It seems there were quite a few people you neglected to tell."

Guilt flooded Rachel. Then fear. This was her worst nightmare come true.

"How did they get to the ranch?" she asked finally. She should have seen this coming. Now that Brett and Gretchen were older, they were bound to try to find out more about their father. But fool that she was, she'd thought she could stave them off with a few vague replies about a marriage that just wasn't meant to be and an early death....

Travis's supercilious look made her want to deck him. "They drove out to the Bar W."

"Drove!"

"Evidently they took off early this morning and got to the ranch about four this afternoon. Walked right up to the front door, introduced themselves to my mother and 'explained' they were doing some 'research' into their roots."

"Oh, my God," Rachel whispered.

"That's right," he thundered, unfolding his frame to stand before her desk. Hands flat on the polished chrome-and-glass surface, he leaned forward until he literally towered over her, all six-foot-four muscle-packed inch of him. He muttered something beneath his breath about crazy, unpredictable women and their gold-digging schemes. "What are you trying to pull here, Rachel?"

"Nothing." She stood and reached for her purse. Her plan set, she strode past him.

He caught her arm as she passed, and reeled her back to his side. "Just where do you think you're going?"

Rachel tried unsuccessfully to shake free of his grip. "Where do you think? To get the twins, of course."

His jaw hardened to the consistency of granite. "I agree that'd be best, and the sooner the better."

Trying hard not to inhale the sexy male scent of him, or notice how thick and glossy and utterly touchable his black hair was, Rachel cast a denigrating look at the hand still curled around her arm. "It'd be a lot easier for me to get out of here if you'd let go."

"Not until we get a few things settled."

"I hardly think—"

"It's an eight-hour drive to the ranch."

Rachel fought the tingles of awareness radiating outward from where he touched her. Using her other hand to pry his fingers from her arm she twisted her body lithely and wiggled out of his grasp. Travis might be wearing a silk tie, but there was still something dangerous and almost disreputable about him. "I remember very well where the ranch is." Her pulse racing, she stalked away from him. "I'll drive all night if I have to."

Travis folded both arms close to his chest. "I have a private jet waiting at the airport. I can get you there in a little over an hour."

The idea of the short travel time appealed to her. The idea of being cooped up with Travis for any length of time, for any reason, did not.

He shrugged his broad shoulders. "Of course if you're afraid to be alone with me..."

She shot him a drop-dead look as they headed for the exit simultaneously. "Don't flatter yourself."

He reached the door first, then stopped and blocked her exit. She backed up and glared up at him, hating his cool superiority almost as much as she hated all the misconceptions she knew he harbored about her.

"So what's your choice, Rachel?" he asked with predatory grace. "Are you going with me or leaving the kids at the ranch for the night?"

Her heart was suddenly beating very fast. And it was all his fault. "That's not a choice," she snapped. "It's a nightmare."

Resting a shoulder against the door frame, he laughed softly. "At least about that much we agree."

As she scanned his face, the bitter memories of her past difficulties with the powerful Westcott family overwhelmed her. And her children, unsuspecting though they might be, were at the center of a newly brewing family storm!

"All right," she said finally, holding his intense blue-gray gaze. She swallowed hard, knowing she had no other choice. "I'll go with you."

THE JET TRAVIS had waiting at the Beaumont airport was small, new and expensive-looking. It was also painted white and red and bore the Texas West Airlines logo. To Rachel, it was the symbol of Travis's almost overwhelming success. In the years since she had known him, he had started his own Texas-based commuter airline and was now a multimillionaire with a national reputation. So the jet itself was no surprise. What she hadn't expected was that Travis was going to pilot it himself.

"Were you at the ranch, too?" Rachel asked as she settled into the seat beside Travis and fastened her seat belt.

"No. I was at my office in Fort Worth when my mother phoned me."

He hadn't lost any time in getting to her, Rachel thought. "Was Jaclyn very upset?"

Travis shrugged. "Not half as upset as she'd be if my father were still alive."

Rachel stared at the instrument panel. "I read about Zeke's death," she said softly. "I'm sorry."

"Are you?" Travis's voice dripped with sarcasm.

Once they took off, Rachel stared out at the fluffy white clouds and sapphire-blue Texas sky. She twisted her hands together in her lap, wishing now as always that Travis wasn't so blunt. Or so hell-bent on calling out the truth, as he saw it, anyway. "You know there was no love between Zeke and me...."

Travis slanted her an aggrieved glance and gave her no chance to continue. "Should there have been?"

"Maybe," Rachel acknowledged tightly. "If he'd ever seen fit to give me a chance."

Travis gripped the controls with both hands. "You proved *your* character the day you eloped with my brother."

His thinly veiled barb was meant to get a reaction and it did. Rachel whirled on him as much as her seat belt would allow. "Did you ever happen to think our marrying might have been Austin's idea?"

"I don't doubt it was." He gave her a scornful once-over, pausing to linger on her breasts, before returning his glance to her eyes. "You were a pretty hot little number even then."

"If you weren't piloting this jet," Rachel fumed, balling her hands into fists, "I'd deck you for that."

One side of his mouth lifted in a taunting smile. "You'll have your chance if you still want it, once we hit the ground. But I warn you—" his silky soft voice sent shivers rolling up and down her spine "—unlike Austin, I fight dirty and I fight to win."

Cheeks flaming, she stared at him in smoldering anger. "I don't doubt that, either," she said.

But the reply she expected never came. He seemed relaxed and completely unperturbed by their argument.

Had she been able to bear the silence, she would have said nothing more the entire rest of the flight. Unfortunately she found the silence worse than their previous repartee. Needing to do something to get her mind off Travis and her potent reaction to him, she said finally, "So, how is your mother?"

Travis continued to concentrate on piloting the small sleek jet. "Happy as a nursing calf now that she thinks she's got a couple of grandchildren. 'Course," he drawled, ignoring Rachel's soft indrawn breath, "I don't know how long that happiness will last." He peered at her contemplatively through twin fringes of narrowed dark lashes. "How long do you think it'll take, Rachel?"

Rachel could tell by the smug look on his face that he was trying to get a rise out of her, but curiosity made her unable to resist taking the bait. "How long for what?" she asked warily.

Both corners of his mouth lifted in a crocodile grin. "For me to expose you."

Rachel shook her head in silent mounting fury. She clamped her arms beneath her breasts and stared straight ahead, damning everyone—the twins, who'd gotten her into this hopelessly untenable position, herself, for foolishly accepting this ride to San Angelo, and Travis, for being so typically rude and insulting. "You're just like your father," she finally said.

"Thanks." He nodded happily, as if she'd just crowned him Prince of Wales. "I appreciate the compliment."

Rachel stared straight ahead. "It wasn't a compliment."

"How come?" he asked innocently.

"You know damn well how come!"

"Tell me, anyway. We've got time to kill."

"Because your father wrecked my marriage to your brother."

"He disapproved," Travis countered argumentatively. "I wouldn't say wrecked."

"Well, I would!" Rachel shot back hotly.

"You're saying you would've stayed married to Austin had my father not disinherited him?"

He took Rachel's silence as a *no*. "Then what are you saying, Rachel?"

Rachel straightened indignantly. "That Zeke's disapproval hurt Austin very much."

"His hasty ill-thought-out marriage to *you* hurt *my father* very much."

"Can we drop this?" she inquired stiffly.

"Sure," he said.

Again, the silence was nearly unbearable. Feeling as wrung out as if she'd just participated in an iron women competition, Rachel sighed. "Whose idea was it for you to come and get me, anyway?" The culprit should be shot at dawn.

"Mine." He grinned at her, enjoying her discomfiture to the hilt. "Regrets?"

Rachel rolled her eyes. "Too numerous to count."

"You'll pardon me if I don't sympathize with you. After all, this scam was not my idea."

"Nor mine," Rachel muttered. He slanted her a doubtful glance. Even though she hated to give it, Rachel knew she owed Travis, indeed the whole Westcott family, an apology for what had happened. "I really am sorry about this," she said.

"Right. And that's supposed to make everything better?" Travis said cynically.

The edge in his voice prompted Rachel to turn and look at him and be confronted almost immediately with how intimate a setting the cockpit of the two-seater jet was.

He had taken off his suit jacket the moment they'd stepped onto the plane, and the striped cotton shirt he wore delineated the muscles of his arms and shoulders, and the washboard flatness of his stomach. She turned her eyes away from the splendid masculinity of his body and back to his face. "This shouldn't have happened," she said firmly.

"I agree with you," Travis said grimly. "The kids never should have driven out to the ranch."

"It's not as if I suggested this to them, Travis!" she retorted.

"Maybe not, but if you had more control over your children, then it wouldn't have happened."

"They're curious about their father."

I am, too, Travis thought, feeling both troubled and irritated. *Was* Austin the twins' father? Or was this all just another one of Rachel's scams? God knew, his mother seemed convinced. They were Austin's spitting image, she'd said. But his mother would have accepted any children claiming to be the offspring of her long-dead eldest son, Travis feared. She wanted Austin back that much. And if not Austin, then some small living part of him. Worse, Travis wanted that, too. Which meant they could both easily be taken for a ride.

"What did you tell the twins about their father?" Travis asked gruffly.

"Only that he died before they were born," she replied in a soft haunted voice.

"And that's it?" Travis asked incredulously. He wished that Rachel had taken the time to change into something less feminine and alluring than the dress she'd worn to work. After all, he had taken her back to her house for an overnight bag.

He wasn't sure what the dress was made of—rayon, maybe—but she couldn't have selected one that would've done a better job of showing off her considerable physical assets had she tried. Both elegant and exotic, the wrap dress molded to her breasts and tied at the side. The full skirt fell almost to her ankles and swirled out from her slim waist when she moved. Even the short cap sleeves revealed the shapely lines of her upper arms. She looked so good in it that whenever Travis looked at her, he felt his mouth water. "In sixteen years, that's all you told them?" he finally managed to say.

"I more or less intimated we had no extended family living. And on my side, anyway, it's true. My dad died a long time ago."

Travis understood why she would've wanted to lie about her own father. In his view, Rachel had plenty to be ashamed of in that regard. What he didn't understand was why she hadn't come to his family. She must have know all along that she could hit on them for financial help. "Why did you lie to them about us?" he asked.

Rachel looked at him as if he were missing a major section of his brain. "Considering the way I was treated by you and your father, like some odious piece of white trash, do you even have to ask?" she snapped.

No, Travis thought, on reflection, he didn't. Had his father known about the twins, had Zeke had even a hint, he would have fought Rachel for custody of Austin's children.

The jet descended through the clouds, and the ranch came into view. Rachel sucked in her breath at the sprawling acreage, with its gentle hills, streams, groves of trees and sprawling pastureland. She had always loved the Bar W Ranch. As a kid, she'd spent hours dreaming about what it would be like to grow up on such majestic land and to command the respect and admiration the Westcotts did. Later, when she and Austin had begun dating, they'd dreamed of living there together. But it wasn't to be.

Travis guided the jet onto the runway. It jolted slightly as the wheels hit, then glided smoothly to a halt. "This wasn't here before, was it?" Rachel asked as they climbed down onto the tarmac.

"No. I had it built after my father died, so I could come home more easily."

Rachel nodded her acknowledgement.

Travis told himself he didn't need her approval as she followed his lead and headed for the pickup truck in the hangar. And yet, irritatingly, it felt good, anyway.

They were both silent as he drove the short distance to the sprawling two-story plantation-style ranch house. Travis could only imagine what Rachel was remembering as she looked at the white stone mansion, with its one-story wings that sprouted on either side of the main house. From an architectural standpoint, the house was perfect in every detail, from the dormer windows on the fashionable gray hip roof to the black shutters that graced both sides of the French doors that doubled as windows for nearly every room. Six white columns supported the wide graceful front porch, and a black wrought-iron railing encompassed the perimeter of the second-floor balcony.

There was a detached ten-car garage. Beyond that was the bunkhouse, the neatly maintained barns and miles of white fence. The house alone was 14,000 square feet. And that didn't count the pool or patios or gardens at the rear.

Most visitors marveled at the sheer beauty of the place. Not Rachel. She seemed to be regarding the sprawling mansion with a mixture of loathing and trepidation. But perhaps that, too, was to be expected, Travis thought. Her single prior visit to the ranch had hardly been a happy one.

Rachel's legs were shaking but she climbed down from the truck as gracefully as she was able and started up the front walk toward the double beveled-glass doors.

She had been to the ranch only one other time, the night Austin had taken her home to announce they

had just eloped. She couldn't help but remember now
how hurt, humiliated and ashamed she had been that
night when she realized she would never be accepted
by Zeke Westcott, Austin's father. He had been so
opposed to their marriage he hadn't even let them get
past the front hall. He'd thrown them out, telling
Austin not to bother to come back until he'd rid himself of his white-trash wife. And Travis, damn him,
had sided with his father. Only Jaclyn Westcott had
ever wanted to give her a chance. . . .

The front doors opened and the welcoming com-
mittee dashed out. "Hey, Mom!" Brett and Gretchen
said simultaneously, hanging back, sheepish looks on
their faces.

Rachel checked them over visually and to her relief
found them none the worse for wear after their unau-
thorized expedition into their past.

"Hello, Rachel," a soft cultured voice said.

Rachel looked up into the eyes of Jaclyn Westcott.
At sixty-two, she seemed frailer, softer. "I hope, now
that we've found one another again, we won't ever lose
touch."

Not sure she knew what the older woman meant and
not sure she wanted to know, Rachel turned to her
children. They might have set out only to satisfy their
curiosity, but now Rachel feared a custody battle, at
the very least a demand for court-dictated visitations
from her late husband's family. She said as pleasantly
but as firmly as possible, "Brett, Gretchen, get your
things together. It's time to go."

"No," Brett said stubbornly, crossing both his arms over his chest. "Gretchen and I have already talked about it. We aren't leaving."

Chapter Two

"It's really nice up here," Rachel said.

Yes, it was, Travis thought resentfully. Thanks to Jaclyn's determined housekeeping, the attic area was spacious, clean and neatly organized. Intrigued with the row of window seats at the dormer windows, Rachel made a beeline for one of them. It was already dark, so she couldn't see much of the ranch below except for the lights lining the front drive. But it was enough to hold her as spellbound as a kid in a candy store, Travis noticed, as he strolled closer.

She turned, nervous now at the idea of being alone with him. Her eyes darted past him to the softly lit attic with its carpeted floor and abundance of storage cabinets and chests. And then back to his motionless form. He knew she was thinking about their errand, which was to bring down slides of the ranch to show the twins, but all he could think about was the irritating intimacy of sitting down to a family-style dinner with Rachel, his mother and the twins. The formal dining room hadn't heard such laughter or activity in years, he realized, not since he and his brother had been kids. Worse, he could see his mother's enchantment with Rachel and her children, and he wasn't one bit comfortable with it. Fortunately the twins weren't interested in the ranch, just in meeting relatives, so they'd be gone soon.

"Can't find the projector?" she asked coolly.

Travis braced a shoulder against the wall, enjoying the way the pulse was beginning to throb at the base of her throat. He let his gaze lazily rove the softness of her lips and tried not to think about how those same lips would feel under his. "I know exactly where it is," he said softly.

Rachel took an uneasy step back. "So what's the problem?" The hollows beneath her cheeks created shadows beneath the paleness of her fair skin.

"No problem," Travis countered laconically, wishing that her hair didn't look so touchable and soft and that she didn't smell quite so good. "I just have a few things to say to you."

"I don't think I want to hear this," she said tersely, starting for the stairs. He moved to block her way. Three steps later, her back was to the attic wall, and he hadn't so much as laid a hand on her. Trapped but not defeated, she lifted her hands to cover her ears. "I'm not going to listen to this," she asserted stubbornly.

"Yes, you will, unless you want my mother to hear it, too."

She evidently knew he meant what he said because she slowly dropped her hands and sent him a murderous look.

"I know what you're up to, Rachel," he informed her flatly. "You're not going to get away with it. Not as long as I have a single breath left in my body."

She smiled at him sarcastically. "I think your death by suffocation could be arranged."

"You wish."

At a stalemate, they stared at one another for long seconds. Long enough for him to see how smooth her mouth was even without lipstick. Long enough for him to see the hot embarrassed color pour back into her cheeks. Their staring match continued. As the moments drew out, he became even more aware of her. His body tightened with pleasure that was almost pain. It was all he could do not to lean in and kiss her smart mouth into stunned silence, just for the sheer hell of seeing her lose her cool.

Rachel's golden eyes widened as if she knew exactly what he was thinking. She tensed, averted her gaze and heaved a bored-sounding sigh. "Okay, Travis," she said, anger giving her voice a taut sexy edge. "You win." She clamped both arms together at her waist and stared at him determinedly. "I'll play your little game. Just what is it you think I'm trying to get away with now?"

"As if you don't know," he said sourly.

"I told you," she said with exaggerated patience. "I don't."

He gave her another long look, letting her know he wasn't fooled for an instant by her innocent act. He stepped closer, so they were mere inches apart now, instead of a foot. "It's very clever, the way you worked it out." Travis dropped his voice to a low predatory whisper and went on with grim admiration, "Sending the kids in first."

"I haven't the slightest idea what you're talking about."

Damn, but she could lie as if it was the truth, he thought. "Don't you?" he asked curtly.

"No." A warning flashed in her golden eyes.

"Then let me enlighten you," he said roughly, advancing closer. The hurt that had been bottled up inside him for years threatened to pour out. His arms shot out to either side of her and he sandwiched her between him and the wall. "You married my brother for his money. After he was disinherited, you left him."

Her expression grew stonier as she elbowed him aside. "His disinheritance had nothing to do with our break-up. I left him because I *wanted* him to reconcile with his family—"

"What a load of bull!" Travis cut her off furiously, not about to let her smooth over what had happened. "You only loved him when you thought you would share in his trust fund and live on this ranch." Didn't Rachel have any idea how much her betrayal of his brother had affected not just Austin, but himself?

For years now Travis had doubted the motives of every woman with whom he came in contact.

"I married Austin because I loved him," Rachel retorted hotly, stepping past him. "And I left him for exactly the same reason."

Travis turned and continued to regard her with contempt. "Some love," he said softly, wondering if Rachel knew how much he had wanted her to prove his father wrong about her, how much he had wanted her to stand by his brother through thick and thin. "The marriage lasted four months."

Rachel held her arms akimbo, as if beseeching him to understand. "We were young. And foolish."

"And selfish," Travis added. His mouth taut, he continued, "Austin was devastated when you walked out on him, so much so that he never recovered." Dammit, his brother had *died,* wanting her back.

"I didn't cause him to drink," she said bitterly. "I didn't put him behind the wheel of that car."

"Didn't you? Funny, I don't remember him ever hitting the bottle *before* he married you."

Tears glistened in her eyes as she whirled on him. "Your family put too much pressure on us—"

"And my mother paid you handsomely to get out—"

"That was after I had left him," she whispered miserably, covering her face with her hands.

"Right," Travis snapped back, irritated that she was actually making him feel some sympathy for her. "It was your reward for a job well done!"

He caught her wrist before she could deliver a stinging blow.

"This is getting us nowhere," she said, twisting free of his grasp.

But there was one more thing Travis had to know. He caught her by the shoulders when she tried to move away. "Answer me this," he demanded roughly as her chest rose and fell with every quick frantic breath. "Did you know you were pregnant with his children when you left him?"

She confronted him with a head-on glare. "No. I never would have left."

He wanted to believe her. He just didn't know if he could or should. She'd duped his family once with her lies. With both his father and his brother gone now, he knew it was up to him to see that she didn't do it again.

TRAVIS WAS in the front hall the following morning when the sound of voices reached him. "Brett and Gretchen may well want to take over the ranch one day," his mother was saying. "Perhaps work it together. But in the meantime, Rachel, I need someone to take over the day-to-day running of it. Since you're the children's mother and Austin's widow, it should be you."

His heart pounding, Travis stayed right where he was.

"I don't know anything about ranching," Rachel protested.

"Neither did I when I married Zeke," his mother countered calmly. "I learned. And I want this ranch to stay in the family."

Deciding this ludicrous conversation had gone far enough, Travis stepped into the room, his temper soaring. He leveled a censuring look at his mother. "Rachel's right, Mother." He cast Rachel a disparaging glance. "She could no more run this ranch than I could sew a dress."

His mother's blue eyes flashed a warning. "You don't know that," Jaclyn countered.

"The hell I don't," Travis retorted sharply. Forcing himself to calm down, he said much more quietly, "Mother, please, stop and think about what you're doing."

"I already have, and my mind is made up. I am deeding the ranch over to Rachel and her children."

"Just like that?" Travis stared at Jaclyn incredulously, wondering if he had ever really known his mother at all.

"Of course not," his mother said. "Rachel will have to prove herself capable of running the ranch first. She'll have three months. If she can keep the ranch running in the black, then the ranch will be hers."

Travis pictured the family wealth going down the drain faster than it could ever hope to be recouped. "And if it's in the red? Then what?" Travis demanded.

"Then I'll figure I'm not cut out for ranching," Rachel cut in.

Travis wheeled on her. To his amazement, she had gotten over her shock and was now siding with his mother. "You can't seriously be thinking of accepting this offer?"

"Only under very specific terms," Rachel replied, looking like the thoughtful competent business-woman she was.

"Which are?" Jaclyn asked, looking pleased.

Rachel folded her arms at her waist and continued in a crisp tone, "One, I be given carte blanche in the running of the ranch. If I'm going to do it, I'll need to do it my way. Two, you'll have to give me time to get everything squared away in Beaumont. Summer vacation is coming up, so it will be no problem to bring the kids out here for the summer. Three, I'll have to take a leave of absence from my job at the travel agency."

Travis stared at her. She was as crazy as his mother. "You're not serious?"

Rachel smiled with deadly calm. Whatever reluctance she had exhibited earlier was gone. "I've never been more serious about anything in my life."

"DON'T LOOK SO SURPRISED to see me," Rachel said.

It had been weeks since she'd accepted Jaclyn's offer. Now she faced an obviously angry Travis.

"Can't help it. I was hoping you'd change your mind," he drawled without apology. He watched her lift a suitcase from her car.

Rachel's jaw set. She was in no mood for this. The drive west had been long and arduous. Fortunately the twins had already gone inside with their grandmother, so they didn't have to witness this. "If you think you're going to spend the next three months haranguing me every single moment we're alone—"

"Gee, Miss Rachel," Travis said sarcastically, "you must read minds because—"

"—you've got another think coming," Rachel continued, oblivious to his interruption.

"—because that's exactly what I planned."

They finished speaking at exactly the same time and stared at one another in silence.

"Keep this up and I'll go to your mother," Rachel seethed.

"Oooh." He spread both his hands and shook them in a parody of a tremble. "I'm a-shaking in my boots."

She swiftly gave him her back and busied herself unloading the car. "You wouldn't want to upset her," Rachel said.

He moved so she could see him. "As far as I'm concerned," he drawled, "*this* is upsetting her."

Rachel set the cardboard box containing her makeup mirror and hot rollers on the hood of the car with a loud thud. "She didn't look upset."

"Give her time." Travis plowed through her belongings, frowning as he looked into the canvas bag containing her electric razor. "I'm sure with you around, she'll get there."

"Look." Rachel slapped his hand away from her toiletries and swung around to face him. "Can't we just give this a chance?" She planted both hands on her slender hips.

He shrugged, slouched against the car and regarded her insolently. "Give me one reason why I should."

His goading brought a warm flush to her face and a burst of adrenaline to her veins. "Family harmony, for one."

Travis rested one elbow on the hood of her car and leisurely crossed his ankles, seeming as relaxed as she was tense. "As far as I'm concerned, you're not family and haven't been for some time," he said pleasantly.

The way he let his eyes rove over her flame-red hair made Rachel wish fervently she could brush her hair so she could restore some order to the wind-tossed curls. "My children are family," she countered, refusing to let him rattle her.

"So?" Travis shrugged indolently before he straightened to his full six-four. "Does that mean you have to be here too?"

She drew a deep breath, fought the flare of her temper and tried one last time to reason with him. "You don't know me very well," she said quietly, the accusation in her voice plain. "But then," she said ever so quietly, "you never did, Travis." She expected him to flinch with guilt at her reprimand. To her disappointment, he didn't move a muscle. "We could change that now," she continued evenly.

"Why would I want to do that?"

She reminded herself that years ago, when she would have welcomed his support, he had sided with his father and stubbornly refused to so much as try to get to know her.

"Because you want things to be different this time," Rachel continued persuasively. "Because you're fair-minded. Or at least you could be..." She knew it in her heart!

He compressed his lips grimly, his conscience remaining unaffected by her impassioned speech. "I also don't want to get burned."

Rachel blew out a long exasperated breath. "You really are just like your father, aren't you?" It wasn't a compliment.

But he took it like one. "To the bone." Travis smiled.

"An advanced chauvinist?"

"And proud of it." He turned back to the car. "Looks like you brought half the house," Travis remarked, moving to help Rachel lift a particularly heavy box from the back seat.

With effort, Rachel turned her glance from his flat stomach. Telling herself it didn't matter how sexy or attractive he was, she kept her voice casually neutral. "Don't tell me that bothers you, too?"

Travis shrugged, and easily pulled out another box she could barely lift. "You're just going to have to take it all back."

"At summer's end?"

He flashed her an unrepentant bad-boy grin. "Or sooner."

Her whole body thrumming with pent-up emotion, she watched him carry a box to the front porch. Striding back to her, his slate-blue eyes boring into hers, he finished in a silken voice that rippled across her skin, warming everywhere it touched. "I don't think you know what you're getting into."

"Being here with you?" she snapped. "I have an idea."

"Sheer hell, huh?" His playful grin said it was otherwise for him. For him, it was beginning to be fun.

"Couldn't get much closer," Rachel affirmed.

His glance swept over her hair, lingered pointedly on her mouth, then returned with lustful abandon to her golden-brown eyes. "You are catching on. But that's not what I was talking about."

"Oh?" She arched a delicate brow.

His handsome face became abruptly serious. "Ranching is a hard life, Rachel."

No, she thought, dealing with Travis was hard. In comparison, ranching would be easy. She sent him a composed smile. "No harder than working for a travel agency or the airlines, I'm sure. Just different. Besides," she said with a wry twist of her mouth, amused he was being so obvious about trying to get rid of her, "it's not as if I'll be taking care of the herd single-handedly, you know."

He didn't find her remark amusing. Stalking closer, he braced his hands on his hips, the movement pushing aside the edges of his suit jacket. "You don't even know how to ride."

"So I'll learn." No matter what Travis did or said in the next few days—and she was sure he would give just about anything a try—he wasn't going to scare her away or stop her from trying to secure her late husband's inheritance for her children.

Travis rubbed a hand along the clean-shaven lines of his jaw. His eyes were intense, and his sensual mouth was mobilized into an even deeper frown. "There's a lot more to it than knowing how to sit a horse," he said as if speaking to a virtual idiot.

He was patronizing her again. "I expect so," Rachel said, mocking his tone to a T.

Their glances did battle silently. "Look," he said reasonably after a moment as he smoothed the thick black hair that grew sleekly down the nape of his neck. "All orneriness aside, I have an idea what this must seem like to you. It's beautiful country out here. And there's no denying the Westcott name carries a lot of clout in this part of Texas. But there the fantasy ends, Rachel," he continued with gruff indifference to her feelings. "You can't just play rancher the way a kid plays house."

Rachel drew a deep breath. Maybe it was good they were getting this all out in the open now. "Are you trying to insult me, Travis, 'cause if you are," she said, making no effort to mask the warning in her low velvet tone, "you're making a good start."

His gaze hardened, letting her know he wouldn't apologize. "I'm trying to be honest with you, Rachel. I thought that was what you'd want."

Rachel walked a distance away, so she wouldn't be inhaling the brisk masculine scent of his hair and skin. "What I want, Travis," she said slowly, enunciating each word and looking directly into his eyes, "is for you to stay the hell out of my way."

Rachel thought but couldn't be sure she saw a glimmer of respect in his eyes.

"I imagine you'll want a few days to settle in before getting involved in the ranch," he said.

"Where are the hired hands?" she asked, the model of polite efficiency. "I'd like to meet them." Maybe if Travis saw she was serious about working hard, he would ease up on her.

Travis grimaced. "This time of day they're all over the place, tending to their chores."

Rachel wasn't buying that. He had to know where someone was. "The chief hired hand, then."

"Our cow boss is Rowdy Haynes," Travis answered carefully.

"You must know where he is," Rachel persisted when no further information was immediately forthcoming.

Again, Travis was silent. He knew but wasn't willing to tell.

"I'd like to meet Mr. Haynes," she continued firmly with a defiant lift of her chin. "The sooner the better." She wished she didn't have to tilt her head so far back to look into Travis's eyes. And wished his black hair wasn't so agreeably tousled by the wind.

Travis shrugged after a moment, his powerful shoulders shadowing her from the worst of the late-afternoon sun. "Have it your way," he said with soft indifference. "As soon as you change I'll—"

Rachel didn't know what Travis had up his sleeve this time, but she wasn't about to give him time to do it, while she was off—just like a woman!—changing her clothes. "That won't be necessary," she interrupted stiffly.

She knew she looked fine in her tailored city shorts and matching pale lemon blazer. She didn't need to put on fresh lipstick to do business. In fact, she felt it would be better if she didn't. Nor would she condescend to the help by putting on jeans and trying to be one of them when undoubtedly they already knew or would soon know, she was not. It would be better just to be herself and let matters progress from there.

Rachel didn't know what to expect when she entered the bunkhouse. A one-room dormitory, maybe. Instead, she saw a dining hall to the left and an office to the right. Straight ahead was a hallway with rooms off to either side.

"The men bunk in the back, two to a room," Travis said. "The showers are at the rear. I wouldn't go back there without an all clear if I were you."

Rachel didn't intend to. Pausing outside the open office door, she glanced in and saw a blond man who couldn't have been more than twenty-five or -six, sitting behind a computer terminal.

"Rowdy, I'd like you to meet my former sister-in-law, Rachel Westcott. She's going to be running the ranch for my mother this summer."

Rowdy's eyes widened speculatively as Travis continued with the quiet authority of a man long accustomed to giving orders, "Starting at 6 a.m. tomorrow, you don't make a move without first consulting her. Mrs. Westcott's to be clued in on every aspect of this ranch. I mean it, Rowdy. You don't make a move before talking to her."

Rowdy absorbed that with a nod. Rachel wasn't quite sure what Travis meant, she only knew she was in trouble. Deep trouble. She swore silently to herself, wishing all the while Rowdy didn't look quite so much as if he was about to burst out laughing.

"Ma'am." Rowdy stood and extended his hand. His brown eyes both questioned Travis and challenged her. "Pleased to meet you."

"I'll be getting settled in today, but first thing tomorrow I expect a tour of the facilities. I also want to see an up-to-date report on every aspect of this ranch."

"Yes, ma'am." Rowdy tried, but didn't quite suppress a smirk before he turned his glance to Travis in a way that was strictly, confidentially, man-to-man. A way that said no matter how well-intentioned Rachel was or how much authority she had she couldn't possibly hope to manage the vast Bar W Ranch.

"You told him not to cooperate with me," Rachel accused the moment she and Travis left the bunkhouse.

Travis shook his head, his mouth grim, and looked at her attentively. "Dream on," he said, the pleasure he felt at his ability to get to her evident.

Rachel reined in her feelings and informed him with icy disdain, "I have a news flash for you, Travis."

He rolled his eyes. "I can't wait."

"I don't care how hard a time he or anyone else gives me. And that includes you. *I'm going to do this. I'm going to succeed!*"

He didn't bother to argue with her, merely lifted a skeptical brow. And although his expression remained disturbingly inscrutable, she had the feeling he was laughing; it rankled, more than she expected.

"Well, don't worry about it. Like my mama said—" Travis rocked back on his heels and stuck his thumbs through the belt loops on either side of his zipper "—you'll get your chance to prove yourself capable. Starting at 6 a.m. tomorrow, Rachel, this ranch is all yours."

"Thank you," she said primly, satisfied he'd finally conceded her this much, however reluctantly.

"What happens after that," he concluded, grinning, "is your problem."

Chapter Three

The alarm went off at five. Rachel slipped out of bed and into the shower. Minutes later, she put on a pair of jeans, boots and a plain blue chambray shirt. She had no idea what a female ranch manager should wear; she only knew she wasn't going back to the bunkhouse dressed in city shorts again.

Slipping silently out of her bedroom, she headed down the hall and out the door. The yard was quiet as she walked over to the bunkhouse. The aroma of coffee wafted out the door.

She knocked briskly on the outer door, then stepped inside. Rowdy's office was empty, but the spacious dining room was not. All conversation ceased the moment she stepped inside. Roughly twenty men sat at the two long tables. It was clear from the empty plates that they'd just finished breakfast

Seeing her, Rowdy stood up. "Boys, this is Miz Westcott," he drawled in a voice as thick and smooth as molasses. "She's going to be running the ranch this summer." To Rachel's relief, there was nothing save the respect due her in his quiet inflection. Apparently he'd had second thoughts since his borderline-rude treatment of her yesterday. Rachel's confidence grew when among the men, there was a murmur of hello.

"I expect she'll want to say a few words," Rowdy said, then sat down.

Actually, Rachel corrected Rowdy silently, she didn't want to speak to the hands, not until she'd had a tour of the ranch and read the reports she'd asked for. But knowing the men were bound to be curious about her, perhaps even nervous about working for someone new, she smiled. "As you all probably have heard by now, this is all new to me, but I expect to get acclimated very quickly. Once I do, I'll undoubtedly be making some changes. I'll expect everyone's full cooperation. In the meantime, if you have any problems or suggestions, please feel free to come to me." She made eye contact with several of the men. "Carry on." She pivoted, intending to head back out the door.

"Uh, whoa, Miz Westcott," Rowdy said, halting her progress.

The undertone of insolent mirth in his voice sent a chill of remorse up her spine. Why, oh why, she thought miserably, had she ever allowed herself to think this was going to be easy?

"What would you like us to work on today?" Rowdy continued in that voice, which was so subservient and overly polite it was rude.

Rachel turned slowly. She had no choice but to play along with Rowdy, but she wouldn't make it easy for him. "Work on?" she repeated mildly.

"Yeah." Rowdy made a great show of trying and failing to suppress a grin before turning abruptly serious. "You want us to move the herds, start branding the new calves or start repairing the fence in pasture forty-one?"

Every man was looking at her, waiting for her to make a mistake. "Split up," she said sternly, giving him a look that said he should be able to figure out some things for himself. "Do all three."

"Can't," Rowdy informed her lazily, shoving his hands deep into the pockets of his jeans. "It'll take every man to move the herds to alternate pastureland."

"Then do that," Rachel said, beginning to feel a little flustered.

"Move them where?" Rowdy asked. "Pasture forty-one is inoperable at the moment." Chagrined, Rachel realized she didn't even know how many pastures the Bar W had.

Drawing on all her inner strength, she regarded Rowdy patiently and willed the embarrassed blush that crept up her neck to stay out of her cheeks. "Where do you usually move them?" she asked.

"Wherever we're told," Rowdy said, beginning to sound as exasperated as Rachel felt.

Rachel took a breath. Fighting panic, she worked on slowing the erratic beat of her pulse. "What other pasturelands are available?'' she asked, keeping her gaze locked on Rowdy.

"She's running this ranch and she doesn't know?" one of the hands muttered incredulously.

"Look, I ain't working for no woman." One of the men in the back stood up, disgruntled. "'Specially not one who doesn't know what the devil she's talking about."

"I agree." Another stood up, then another and another.

"Wait a minute," Rachel said, desperately trying to stave off disaster. "All of you worked for Jaclyn Westcott."

"That's different," another man in the back spoke up. "*She* knows what the hell's going on."

"Well, I will, too," Rachel asserted bravely.

"When?" one of the hands, a grizzled-looking man with three days' growth of beard, asked in disgust. "I vote we strike. Or at least put Rowdy in charge."

Rachel looked at Rowdy, expecting him to help her out, now that the joke was over and they had indeed initiated her by fire, but all he did was shrug. He looked at her as if to say, *what the hell did you expect, lady?*

The men started filing out the door.

Rachel was so angry she was tempted to just let them quit, but she knew she couldn't. Jaclyn had already told her the Bar W had the best hands for miles around. Rachel *might* be able to succeed without them, but having them quit on her first day was the kind of start she didn't need. Besides, she knew that the only way she could learn the business was if they were there to help her.

"Hold it," Rachel said. When that didn't stop them, she put two fingers in her mouth and whistled shrilly. The men stopped walking but continued to talk. She stepped up on a bench and regarded them from a position of physical superiority.

The dissenting voices of the men slowly quieted and silence reined in the room. "Let's talk about this," she said, her years of negotiating difficult travel packages for individuals and corporations coming to her aid. "Exactly what would get you to stay?" she asked flatly.

"More money," the grizzled cowpoke said.

Then money it was, Rachel thought, not daring to think how this was likely to be received by Travis when he found out. If he found out. "How about a ten percent raise, effective immediately?"

The men no longer looked ready to walk, neither did they look ready to give in. "And another ten percent for every man who's still here, working hard, at the end of the summer."

She had them. She knew it by the slow smiles that spread across their faces.

"All right then, that's settled. Now, I need someone to help me determine the daily schedule. If not Rowdy, then—"

Rowdy interrupted. "I can do that."

Rachel knew Rowdy was only volunteering to avoid giving up power. He was still going to be trouble. Like Travis, he just didn't want her here. Still, she'd succeeded where she wasn't wanted before. Maybe not when she was married to Austin, but plenty of times since. "You think you can handle things for today?" she said curtly, making it clear she wasn't awarding him the job indefinitely, not unless his attitude changed.

Rowdy was cooperative but not defeated. "Yes, ma'am, I reckon I can," he responded tersely.

This once, Rachel decided she could ignore the insolence in Rowdy's brown eyes. But she'd be damned if she'd do so three days from now. She'd fire the son of a gun, rather than work with a thorn in her side. "Fine. I'll see you all tomorrow." She stepped down from the bench unassisted, turned on her heel and left.

Rachel was still shaking with the emotional ordeal of the narrowly averted strike as she slipped in the front door of the ranch house and saw Jaclyn fussing over the sideboard in the dining room. Travis was beside her, helping himself to a cup of coffee. For someone who didn't live at the ranch anymore, Rachel thought sourly, he was sure around a lot. Worse, he was dressed in a pair of jeans that did amazing things for his rear end and a cotton shirt that outlined the contours of his chest to mouth-watering effect, which meant he probably was not planning to go to his airlines office in Fort Worth today.

"Rachel, where have you been so early?" Jaclyn asked.

"Speaking with the hands." Rachel helped herself to a plate and steadfastly avoided Travis's gaze. She began helping herself to ham and eggs. What did it matter to her how wickedly attractive he looked in jeans? "We were going over their work assignments for the day."

Jaclyn started. "Already? I didn't know you intended to get started so soon, or else we would have talked!"

Rachel smelled a rat. Jaclyn turned to her son, her displeasure with him evident. "I told you I wanted Rachel to wait until next week before she dealt with the hands."

"It wasn't up to me." Travis shrugged. "Rachel wanted to get started right away."

More likely I was pushed into it, Rachel thought.

Jaclyn shook her head in regret. "I'm sorry, Rachel," she said, as she took a seat at the head of the table. "This is my fault. I was so preoccupied helping the twins get settled in yesterday, I didn't think to discuss my plans for the transition with you."

You mean there were some? Rachel thought, weak with relief. Maybe this wouldn't be such an impossible task, after all. "That's all right," Rachel soothed, grateful she had Jaclyn on her side. "Travis was more than helpful." She turned so only he could see her dagger-filled look. *I'll pay you back for this, Travis,* she thought, and felt a jolt of satisfaction when he had the conscience to look uncomfortable.

"It went well?" Jaclyn asked hopefully.

Rachel would tell Jaclyn about the threatened strike, but not with Travis sitting there so smugly. "It went fine," she lied. "But I can see I've got my work cut out for me." She turned so she couldn't see Travis at all. "You'll help me get situated?"

"Of course, dear. I wouldn't dream of throwing you into this with no preparation," Jaclyn said.

But Travis would, Rachel thought grimly, which pointed up sharply the difference between the Westcott men and the Westcott women.

HOURS LATER, Travis was driving around the ranch, checking on both the property and the herd and making notes about things to tell Rowdy on the sly. Fortunately he'd had the foresight to arrange to take the whole week off. And it was a good thing, too, considering the way things were shaping up. He'd half expected Rachel to back out of her agreement by now. She hadn't.

Needing a break, he cut the engine on the pickup and got out to look at the rolling green hills and acres of painted white fence. Funny, he hadn't actually lived on the ranch for years, yet the idea it would not be his made his gut twist painfully. For as long as he could remember, this had been his home, his center. He ate and slept in a condo in Fort Worth, but this was still where his heart was and always would be. And dammit, his mother knew that.

There wasn't an acre of land here that didn't hold some memory for him. He could hardly drive half a mile without seeing where he'd first learned to ride, or first been thrown, or where he and Austin had played and fought. Brothers. Heart and soul.

Oh, he knew why his mother was doing this. She felt guilty. So did he. Because neither of them had been able to stand up to Zeke. He certainly hadn't been able to get his stubborn cuss of a father to stop riding Austin so hard, though God knew he had tried to divert Zeke's attention from his older brother. But Austin was all his father had ever been able to focus on. It had been Austin upon whom Zeke had pinned all his dreams. Travis didn't know if it was because Austin was his firstborn, or if Zeke just liked him better. He only knew that he had paled in comparison to his brother, at least in his father's estimation. And if he let his mother hand over the ranch to Rachel, he would've failed again. Miserably.

He just wished it wasn't going to be so tough to take the place away from her. Because he knew now, if he hadn't before, just how hard and long she intended to fight him.

Unfortunately, no sooner had Travis returned to the ranch house than he was confronted by his mother. One look at her face and he knew she was furious with him.

"You get those hands in line, Travis, or I swear I'll fire every one of them."

Travis felt a flicker of hope. He'd been wondering all day what had happened down at the bunkhouse. It seemed he was about to find out. "Did Rachel tell you they gave her a hard time?" he asked innocently.

"She didn't have to," his mother stormed. "I saw how pale and defeated she looked this morning."

Travis had seen it, too. Remembering, he was overcome with guilt. He could have smoothed the way by introducing Rachel in such a way that she would have been accepted, but he hadn't. Because he knew, as surely as Rowdy and the others hands did, that Rachel didn't belong there. She would never be able to run the ranch, not the way his father had, or his mother after Zeke died.

Travis went to the refrigerator and helped himself to a long-necked beer. "I can't fire Rowdy. We need him too badly."

"Another cow boss could be found. A former daughter-in-law and twin grandchildren cannot."

Travis studied his mother. "You're doing this for Austin, aren't you?" But Rachel had left Austin, and Travis didn't intend to let her disgrace or hurt the family again.

"And myself. Every time I look at them, it's like having a second chance with your brother." She came toward him and touched her hand to his arm. "Don't you understand that, Travis?"

Travis was beginning to.

His mother shook an admonishing finger at him. "If you can't help Rachel, at the very least stay out of her way. I mean it, Travis. I lost my eldest son because Zeke wouldn't welcome Rachel into his heart and his home. I will not lose my grandchildren because of you."

HOURS LATER, an exhausted Rachel slumped over the desk in the study that had once belonged to Zeke. Running the Bar W was a bigger job than she had ever imagined, but Jaclyn had gone overboard to help her, giving her a computer-generated list of things that had to be done daily, such as the feeding. Weekly, she had the payroll. Monthly, ordering food for the bunkhouse and arranging visits from the vet. Quarterly, filing income-tax returns. Now Rachel not only knew what to do, but when to do it.

In addition, she had read the personnel files on every hand, as well as a brief overview of the various problems they'd had since Jaclyn had taken over management. Next on her list was a stack of ranching journals that explained current breeding practices. She would not return to the bunkhouse until she had a handle on that. As soon as she did, and she was coming closer with every hour that passed, she would ask to be taken on a tour. From there, she would—

Rachel's thoughts were rudely interrupted. The door to Zeke's study was flung open and Travis stormed in. "Who the hell authorized you to give the hands a twenty percent raise?"

She had known this was coming. Rachel stood so she could face him on eye level. "Your mother did."

Travis wasn't the slightest bit appeased. He stalked forward. "Does she *know* about it?" he asked, his blue-gray eyes as hard as glass.

"As a matter of fact," she said proudly, "she does, Travis. In fact, we had a long talk about it this afternoon. *She* thought I should have fired the hands outright for insubordination, but I didn't want to do that, not until I'd given them a chance to get to know me and correct their behavior."

"We'll go broke before that happens," Travis fumed.

"I don't think so. I've looked at the books, Travis. This ranch operates in the black by a wide margin."

"Not for long," Travis predicted direly. He slouched in one of the leather wing chairs in front of Zeke's old mahogany desk. "Not the way you do business."

Just as Travis's attitude was entirely too bleak and forbidding, this room was entirely too dark and gloomy, Rachel thought, getting up to move around.

She turned toward him, sending him her most censorious look. "You're right," she said smoothly. "I shouldn't have had to give the hands a ten percent raise to stay on, or another ten as incentive to last out the summer, and it probably wouldn't have been necessary if you'd done a better job handing over the reins. Instead you treated me like some interloper—"

"Which you are," he interrupted crudely.

"—who has no business being here," Rachel continued, ignoring his interruption. She stalked close, her heels moving soundlessly across the faded red Persian carpet. "The hands merely responded in kind—"

Travis swore virulently. He got up and sent his black Stetson hat sailing across the room. It hit the heavy red velvet draperies and fell to the floor with a muffled thud. "You gave them a raise for that?" he countered furiously.

Rachel turned and gave the hat a lengthy perusal, letting him know without saying a word how childish she found that particular gesture. She turned back to him, her composure intact. He had rattled her but good the day before, almost ruining her relationship with the hired hands before it began. She wouldn't give him license to do so again. "I gave them a raise to stop them from going on strike," she said plainly, holding his lancing gaze with very little effort, so virulent was her own anger.

Knowing she was going to lose her temper, too, if she didn't rein in her feelings, she lowered her voice. "I had to give them a raise. The ranch can't afford to be without good help, and I don't yet have the expertise to be able to hire replacement hands. *Yet,*" she said with icy determination. "In three months, if they're still giving me a hard time, they'll be out on their butts." *You, too.*

Travis swore again. He stomped over to retrieve his Stetson, as if he had no idea how it got there. "I knew this was going to cost us." He whacked the hat against his thigh before shoving it back on his head. "I just didn't know how much."

She wasn't sure if he was talking about the past or the present. But it didn't matter what he thought of her then, and it didn't matter what he thought of her now. "Is that all?" she asked coolly, more anxious for him to leave than he would ever know.

"No, it's not all." Tipping his hat back on his head with an index finger, he came toward her, not pausing until they were a scant twelve inches apart. "Before you do something like this again, you clear it with me."

"When, may I ask?" she countered, and had the pleasure of seeing his eyes darken. "On one of your infrequent visits to the ranch?"

Travis stepped nearer, until the distance between them had completely closed and they stood toe-to-toe. She inhaled the rich masculine scent of him, felt the warmth of his body and saw the muted desire in his eyes.

"As it happens," he said ever so softly, his well-thought-out words sending chills of sensual awareness racing up and down her spine, "you'll have plenty of time to see me. I'm moving back in."

Chapter Four

"You can't do that," Rachel said.

"The hell I can't!" Travis shot back smugly.

"You have a business in Fort Worth."

"Yes, I know," he retorted dryly.

"And a condo."

"And a fax and a phone and a computer," he finished her recitation for her impatiently. His eyes narrowed beneath the shelf of his thick black brows. "I'll be bringing them all here." Seeing her displeasure at the news, one side of his mouth lifted in a taunting grin. "Which isn't to say I won't occasionally have to fly into Fort Worth for the day," he admitted with comically exaggerated regret, "but the rest of the time, Rachel darling, I'm going to be here. What do you think about that?"

"You don't want to know."

"Maybe I do," he returned smoothly. In an effort to avoid physical contact with him, she stepped back. Her hips hit the edge of the desk with an unexpected thud, knocking books and papers every which way.

Travis reacted with damnable swiftness, reaching forward to keep her ranching books from sliding to the floor with his right hand and catching a wealth of computer printouts with his left. He shoved them back onto the desk, then instead of stepping back, as any gentleman would have, he planted his hands on either side of her, the warm sides of his palms and his thumbs touching the sides of her hips.

"I'm waiting," he provoked softly.

And I'm determined not to play. Her head tilted back. Refusing to let him badger her into compliance, or harass her off the ranch, she merely lifted an unimpressed brow. "Is this really necessary?"

"I don't know," he replied, his gaze roving her face. "Suppose you tell me."

"I'm not telling you anything except to buzz off," Rachel muttered, planting a hand in the middle of his chest. She pushed. He went nowhere. Not about to engage in an undignified struggle with him, she merely glared at him stonily and prepared to wait him out. Surely he would tire of this intimidation routine soon.

"And that you're incorrigible," Rachel couldn't help but add as the seconds ticked by.

"Thanks." He grinned.

"Not to mention rude—"

"Don't forget opinionated—" he drawled.

"Chauvinistic—"

"And determined," he added, shifting his weight so his knees nudged hers. Seductively. Unbearably. "Don't forget that."

"I won't," Rachel muttered, moving her legs slightly to avoid further contact with the warm solidness of his. It was a mistake. No sooner had she shifted than he used her momentary imbalance to wedge a space between her jean-clad legs and push even closer. To her mortification and fury, he didn't stop until the outsides of his thighs nudged the insides of hers. Streamers of electricity sparked everywhere they touched, adding to the weightless feel in her tummy. And though they still weren't touching *there,* she could imagine all too potently what it would feel like if they were.

And that was when he did it. Simply lowered his mouth to hers. Fit his lips over hers. And kissed her.

Lord, could the man kiss. She'd never felt such a swirling of emotion. She was consumed with heat as he kissed her long and hard and deep. Her head was swimming. Her heart soaring. Her conscience...

Her conscience! Oh, hell! she thought as she regained her senses.

Drawing back, she slapped him. Hard. He wasn't the least deterred.

Palms flat on the desk on either side of her, he leaned even closer, the faint rasp of his evening beard briefly scoring her cheek. "So what do you think, Miss Rachel?" he whispered, his warm breath fanning her hair. "Are you going to enjoy being so close to me day and night, night and day?"

Rachel held perfectly still. He was dauntingly close to her, close enough to easily turn this confrontation into either a wrestling match she was bound to lose or yet another searing soul-numbing kiss. "You know I won't," she predicted darkly, glaring at him, daring him to give her another reason to slap him. "But you should also know I don't plan to capitulate no matter how unpleasant you try to make my stay."

"Is that so?"

"Yes." She was determined not to let him know how disturbing she found his continued closeness, but she could do nothing about the frantic beating of her heart. "And just for the record..." she continued silkily.

"Yes?"

She smiled and looked straight into his eyes. "I think you're a woman-chasing chauvinistic jerk."

He laughed, soft and low. Too late, Rachel realized that by losing her temper, even slightly, she had fallen into his velvet-lined trap. But not for long, she vowed silently.

"Not that it matters to me what you do," she continued coolly. Palm to his chest, she shoved him out of her way and continued around to the other side of her desk. Her golden eyes radiated a warning. "So long as you stay out of my way."

"Think again, sweetheart." Travis waited until she'd sat down again, then sent her a crocodile smile. "I plan to be underfoot all the time. In fact, I'll be around so much it'll probably be downright aggravating."

"Suit yourself." Rachel went back to the papers on her desk. She had tons of literature from the Texas A&M University extension service to go through. It didn't matter to her if he wanted to stay and watch. She just hoped he wouldn't try to kiss her again.

"And I'll be taking back this office, too," Travis said.

Her head snapped up. Her full attention captured once again, she stared at him, seething. He knew damn well this office was the main symbol of power at the ranch and had been for years. Whoever occupied it was deemed to be in charge. If he took it over, then the men, Rowdy especially, would assume that Travis was still in charge, regardless of Jaclyn's decision.

"We'll see about that," she said.

He tipped his hat at her in a way that promised only more devilment. "We certainly will," he promised smoothly.

IT WAS AFTER MIDNIGHT the next evening when Travis came into the house carrying his fax machine. Pausing only to turn on the hall light, he nudged one of the double oak doors open with the toe of his boot and strode into the study. He'd intended to set the fax down on the top of the desk, but the desk wasn't where it should have been. Swearing, he set the machine on the floor, then backed cautiously to his left and reached for the light switch.

He was still swearing two minutes later when a smug-looking Rachel sauntered in. "Back already?" she asked sweetly.

"What the hell have you done?" he thundered, looking at the sleek ultramodern office furniture. The room was done over in pearl gray and pale peach.

"What does it look like I've done?" Rachel glanced around as proudly as an interior decorator. "I've made this office my own."

He curtailed the urge to cross the room, toss her over his shoulder and haul her upside down to her car. "Where's the furniture that used to be here? That's *always* been here?"

"In the sewing room off the kitchen. Your mother said you could set up shop there. She thought you'd prefer it to one of the upstairs bedrooms but—"

"What I would prefer," he interrupted through clenched teeth, "is this room. With everything as it was."

"Sorry." Rachel paraded past him. Taking a seat behind her new desk, she crossed her legs demurely at the ankle and tugged at the hem of her trim ladylike skirt. "But I've taken over in here."

"So I see," he said grimly. "But not for long."

Her chin went up. She shot him a victorious smirk. "That's what you think."

He studied her, searching for a raw nerve, a way to recapture his advantage. But all he saw was a hauntingly beautiful face, a nose that was as slim and straight and impertinent as the rest of her, golden eyes that radiated intelligence, and lips that were so sensual and compelling they bordered on being downright voluptuous. Worse, she harbored an innate determination to have her own way and an inner drive and ambition every bit as strong as his own.

But he couldn't let any of that sway him from what he had to do. His gaze swept the sexy disarray of her flame-red curls. "I'm not going to make this easy for you, Rachel. I'm not just giving you the ranch."

She rolled her eyes in a parody of surprise. "Honestly, Trav, I never would have guessed."

"You may have conned my mother and made her feel guilty for the family's actions years ago—"

"But not you," Rachel guessed. She rested her chin on her hand.

"No, not me," he confirmed flatly, not about to let his head be turned by a pretty face and an even prettier body. "I know your marriage to my brother was a mistake."

Her eyes flashed and she leapt to her feet, closing the distance between them. "Maybe it was," she asserted, her temper flaring. "Maybe we weren't strong enough then, either of us. But I'm strong enough now, Travis." She shook her index finger at him like a teacher chastising an errant student. "Strong enough to stand up to you and Rowdy and anyone else who might get in the way of my doing what is best for my kids."

He caught her hand and pushed it down between them. "And what's that?" he asked silkily.

She wrested her hand from his light grip and stepped back, her breasts heaving. "Giving them a sense of their father and the heritage he would've wanted them to have."

Travis tore his eyes from her chest. "And the Westcott money has nothing to do with it," he said sarcastically.

"Wrong again!" Rachel snapped. "The Westcott money has everything to do with it. Because you see, Travis, I learned long ago, that without money, there is very little freedom." Her voice dripped to a compelling whisper. "And what I want most for my children is the freedom to choose ... to be anything they want to be."

Looking at her, he could almost believe it. Almost.

Dammit. Hadn't he promised himself he wouldn't let her con his family again? And here he was, almost falling for her latest scam.

He looked around the office again. "I'll get even with you for this," he swore. And it was a promise he meant to keep.

"YOU'RE SWINGING the rope too low. You need to hold it higher. Over your head, not level with it."

Rachel turned to see Travis propped up negligently against the corral fence. His powerful body was silhouetted against the midmorning sun. The temperature was already ninety and inching higher. She had started perspiring hours ago, but Travis looked cool and relaxed. His jeans cloaked his powerful calves and

thighs and pinpointed his abundant sex with disturbing accuracy. Her resentment of him upped another
notch. "Go away."

He laughed at her low succinct tone and sauntered
nearer, his boots rhythmically kicking up clouds of
dust. "Can't take a little friendly criticism?"

"I can't take you," Rachel corrected, refusing to
notice that he smelled like soap, leather and expensive cologne and that his eyes lazily cataloged the
sweat-stained fabric of her shirt. Irritated by the way
her clothes kept sticking damply to her chest, Rachel
lifted the lasso and took another practice swing.
"Now, goodbye, Travis."

"Who's been teaching you?" he asked curiously.

"Why do you care?" Rachel asked as the rope circled overhead once, twice, then caught on her hair.

"'Cause I do." Wordlessly he extricated the loop of
rope from her hair. His teeth flashed white in his suntanned face. "Cowboying isn't as easy as it looks, is
it?" he taunted.

Rachel tossed her head impatiently. "Easier than
dealing with the likes of you."

The impact of her insult didn't register on his face.
"Try it again," he instructed inscrutably.

"Not until you leave."

He hooked his thumbs through his belt loops and
rocked back on his heels. "Afraid you'll miss in front
of me again, huh?"

"No. Afraid I won't be able to quell the impulse to
lasso *you*."

"Yeah?" To her mounting fury, he looked intrigued by the thought.

"And," Rachel continued archly, wishing just once she could get the better of him, "tighten the noose."

Rather than be infuriated with her as she had wanted, he threw back his head and laughed. The sound of his rich masculine voice echoing in the stillness infuriated her even more than his irksome presence. Determined to show him she was more of a rancher that he thought, she aimed her lasso. It swung high and wide and landed, with miraculous accuracy, on the target she'd sought.

"Okay. So now you've managed to lasso a fence post," Travis drawled from close behind her. "Let's try something harder. Something that moves," he said as she marched forward to extricate her rope from the post.

"Fine." Rachel pushed the word between gritted teeth and shot him a deadpan look meant to provoke. "Go get me a cow, Travis, and I'll lasso it."

"One of those new organically raised Brahma ones you just bought?"

Rachel stopped dead in her tracks. Was there anything he didn't know about her actions? "How'd you hear about that?" she ground out suspiciously.

"Oh, it's the talk of the ranch," he assured her confidently. "Not to mention the entire county."

She surveyed him grimly. "Why?"

"'Cause they're more expensive to purchase and to raise, for starters." Travis sauntered closer. He pushed his hat back, so she could better see his face. "I don't know what they taught you at the ranch-management seminar you just took over at Texas A&M, sugar, but there's very little market for organically raised beef. In fact, I know of only two supermarkets in the entire state that even carry it."

She sent him a haughty look. "On the contrary, Travis, there's a big demand, but there are only two major *sources* to supply it. I intend to make our ranch the third."

Travis braced his legs apart and crossed his arms over his chest like a bandit about to embark on a raid. His eyes narrowed. "Have you discussed any of this with my mother?"

"Yes." Rachel smiled at him sweetly. "She thinks it's a great idea."

Travis's jaw clenched in a way that filled Rachel with satisfaction. "I suppose you told her how much harder it will be to raise this beef?"

Telling herself it was only fair to give him as much grief as he was giving her, Rachel busied herself rewinding her rope and shrugged off his cautionary words. "It's not that much harder," she replied. "I just have to see that they're fed organically grown grain, and water that's free of any pesticides, fertilizers and herbicide runoff."

"The calves can't be fed any growth hormones—"

"The Bar W doesn't use steroids to begin with."

"—or antibiotics or parasiticides," Travis said, anticipating her side of the argument lazily as he followed her back toward the center of the corral. "What are you going to do if one of the calves gets sick?"

"I'll call Doc Harvey and have him promptly remove it from the herd. It can still be treated, Travis."

"But no longer sold as organic," Travis argued, wondering if she had any idea just how good she looked in those jeans. They hugged her fanny just right and made the most of her long slim thighs, clinging until they disappeared into the half-moon tops of her calf-high red boots.

"True, but then it could be put in with the rest of the herd and sold on the commercial market," Rachel said, lifting her face to his.

"Not at a profit," he said, staring down into her golden-brown eyes. He shouldn't have kissed her the other night. He knew it. It had just been a power play on his part, meant to startle or scare or goad her into packing up and leaving. It hadn't worked. And ever since, he'd not been able to get her out of his mind or forget how sweet her lips had tasted. He hadn't been able to stop himself from wanting more. And that left him with only one recourse. He had to do everything in his power to get her off this damn ranch before he started something and before she surrendered. Because that would make their current harassment of each other seem penny-ante.

"So, yes, it'll be more expensive to raise cattle this way," Rachel continued, "but we'll get more for our money in the end."

Travis put a hand on her elbow and turned her toward him. "You really think you know what you're doing," he said grimly, knowing even if she thought she did that she didn't.

"Yes," she said confidently, her head high. "I do. Your mother and I both think this is the way to go. We're starting small, of course, to work out the kinks, but if it's successful, we'll be changing the whole operation over the next three years, until the Bar W is raising only organic beef."

Travis knew Rachel's plan sounded good on paper. But in reality there was much that could go wrong. He shrugged. "It's your funeral."

"Thanks," she said, extricating her elbow from his grasp. "I appreciate that."

He paused.

"Something else on your mind?" she prodded. "As long as we're having this discussion, we might as well get it all out in the open." When he didn't respond, she strode away from him.

It wasn't his job to protect her. Travis fought the reflexive chivalrous need to step in. Wasn't this exactly what he wanted? For her to make so many mistakes so quickly that his mother would have no choice but to take back control?

It was and it wasn't. Oddly enough, he didn't want to see her hurt. Not that way, anyway. Not when he knew she was trying so hard. He hadn't expected that. He wasn't quite sure what he had expected. Maybe for her to be some sort of behind-the-desk ranch manager who'd taken on airs. Instead, she was out with the men more often than not. She'd made no secret that she was learning the business and she welcomed all help. And because she was so pretty and sociable, she got plenty from some of the younger men.

Of course most of the men still resented her. But he had the uncomfortable feeling that would pass, given time and continued hard work on her part. It was her feelings for him that were harder to deal with.

She detested him. That was never clearer than now, with her glaring feistily at him from across the corral. Of course maybe he deserved that, considering the way he'd treated her. But she was an interloper, he reminded himself sternly.

Still, he shouldn't have kissed her. He'd just done it to get a rise out of her, to shut her up and watch her eyes light up with fiery temper. But it had been so good he hadn't even minded the slap. So good he was still thinking about it, wishing he could haul her into his arms and do it again right now. And that, he knew, wouldn't do. Not if he wanted her off this ranch.

Travis followed her. "There's nothing on my mind but lassoing," he said, picking up their earlier discussion. "Now that you've mastered the fine art of capturing fence posts, you really should try something harder."

"I said I'd be happy to lasso you," she returned.

He grinned, liking the way the color flooded her fair cheeks. "Go ahead and try it."

Looking at him standing there so arrogantly with his arms over his chest, his legs braced apart, his black Stetson low over his brow, Rachel wanted nothing more than to put him in his place once and for all. She shot him a dark look. "My pleasure, cowboy," she drawled.

She swung the rope, aimed it and threw. He moved. The rope landed in the dirt.

"Missed," he pointed out cheerfully, looking as contrarily pleased with her ineptness as she was frustrated by it.

"You moved," she accused angrily, reeling in her rope with swift jerky motions.

"So do cows," he pointed out affably.

She swung again, fast and hard, hoping to catch him off guard. He caught the rope with one hand and with a light yank reeled *her* in, fast and hard. "Like to play rough, huh?" he taunted. "So do I."

Her breath was coming in quick shallow pants. "It doesn't matter how much you harass or belittle me, Travis. I'm not leaving."

He caught her to him, so their legs and stomachs were aligned. "It can get very hot out here in the summer," he warned softly as his eyes drifted over her face. "Too hot for some."

Her breasts rose and fell with each agitated breath. "Then you better head for the air-conditioning, Travis," she countered just as softly, dimly aware that she had never felt more alive in her life than she did at that very moment. "'Cause I love the heat."

His eyes darkened. His head lowered. His lips parted. For one long moment she had the oddest sensation he was going to kiss her again. She told herself firmly to lean back, but instead found herself leaning toward him....

He released her so swiftly she nearly lost her balance. "I love the heat, too, sugar." His low voice vibrated with promise and passion. His eyes sparkled with mischief and desire. "So watch out." On that note, he grinned at her, tipped his hat and sauntered away.

Fuming silently, the lasso clutched tightly in her gloved palm, she watched him swagger toward the gate. It wasn't fair, she thought, that one man should have so much. He was handsome, intelligent, irksome as all get out and arrogant to a fault. Plus, he had a will and inner determination that was surely as strong as hers.

But he was wrong about her.

She did belong on this ranch. And so did her children. And one day soon she would prove it to him.

Chapter Five

"Planning a ride?" Travis asked from the other end of the stables, several days later.

"No, I'm just practicing saddling this horse," Rachel responded ironically. Since the lassoing "lesson" she had avoided him steadfastly, seeing him only at family dinners. But it seemed her luck had run out, as she had known in her heart, it eventually would. No matter how much Travis swore he detested her, he just couldn't stay away from her for long.

"Where're you going?"

Unable to help but note how ruggedly fit and handsome he looked in his faded jeans and dark blue denim shirt with the pearl snap buttons, his Stetson pulled low across his brow, Rachel leaned beneath the horse and finished tightening the cinch. Initially, she had no plans of answering him. But it seemed he wasn't going to budge until she satisfied his curiosity, at least marginally. "Out," she said.

He grinned, as if knowing just how much he annoyed her.

"Out where?" he prodded.

"Out to check on my new Brahma calves."

"Right." He gave a mock serious nod. "The organically raised folly."

"Very funny."

"I doubt you'll think so when you see what effect raising them has on the ranch books. Especially when you add that to the raise you already gave the hired hands. There's going to be one big addition in the debit column."

Rachel was already uneasily aware of that. She'd initially done too much too fast, but as it was too late to go back and undo anything, she knew she would just have to muddle through and find a way to make everything work. She knew she could. She just had to apply herself and not let Travis's constant taunting and chaperoning get the better of her. "Must you constantly interfere?" she asked, regarding him as if he were a loathsome snake.

He straightened with an indolent shrug. "I thought I was trying to help."

Rachel swung herself up into the saddle. It took her only a moment to get her weight situated in the middle, but she could have sworn he was laughing at her from behind the palm he speculatively ran across his jaw. To his credit, however, his blue eyes were serious as he met hers.

His dark brows drew together. "You sure you know what you're doing?" he asked, unable to completely mask his worry over her safety.

"I think I can ride a mile to the pasture without getting lost," Rachel retorted stiffly, trying not to notice just how far she was from the ground, now that she was sitting astride her mount. Or let on how much that still bothered her.

Travis's eyes sized her up. "You ever been out entirely on your own?" he pressed.

"Of course I have," Rachel replied, ignoring the real thrust of his question. "I drive around the ranch in my pickup all the time. In fact, I have now not only memorized most of the pastures, but I know where all the gates for each are located, too."

"I meant on the back of the horse," Travis persisted.

Rachel was miffed he was still dwelling on what she had yet to learn, rather than what she had already accomplished. "I'll be fine." It was time she went out without Rowdy anyway.

Rachel put a rein in each of her hands. She tapped her horse lightly in the sides with the heels of her boots. To her humiliation, the horse refused to move. She tried again, a little harder this time. Still no luck.

Travis rolled his eyes and shook his head. "Given that demonstration of your expertise, there's no way you're going out alone," he muttered.

Ignoring her prompt protests, he grabbed a saddle and threw it on the back of his own horse. In a tenth the time it had taken her to saddle up, he was finished and leading his horse by the reins out into the walkway in the center of the stables beside hers.

"This really isn't necessary," Rachel said.

"The hell it isn't," Travis said roughly, halting his horse right next to hers. He held her eyes for a breath-stealing moment before continuing in a low soft penitent voice, "My mother'd have my hide if I let anything happen to you. Besides—" he grinned, leaning over and taking her reins "—this horse is a valuable animal. Don't want anything happening to it."

Rachel resisted the urge to call him a few colorful names as, astride his horse, he led hers out of the barn.

"How did you do that?" Rachel asked, frowning, as she began to bump along in the saddle with an uneven rhythm. Beside her, Travis moved smoothly, one with his horse.

"Do what?" he retorted.

"Get my horse to go?" Rachel asked, frowning again, wondering what she'd forgotten. She was sure she'd done everything Rowdy'd taught her to do.

"You were holding the reins too tight," Travis supplied, telling both horses, "Whoa." He swung himself out of the saddle and opened the corral gate. "Pulling on the reins means stop."

"Yes, I know that," Rachel grumbled, wishing he didn't make everything she found so difficult about riding, beginning with getting on and off a horse, look so darned easy, as easy as breathing.

"Figured you did." He grinned at her from beneath the brim of his hat, and once they had cleared the corrals and were headed off toward the pasture and her young Brahma herd, he bent over and handed the

reins back to her. Leaning back so that his weight was
situated squarely in his saddle, he glanced at her speculatively. "You always bounce around in the saddle
like that?"

Rachel rolled her eyes. If he'd been any kind of
gentleman at all, he wouldn't have commented on her
lack of expertise. "I'm still learning." She jerked up
and down, up and down, her bottom smartly hitting
the saddle with every step.

"Yeah. I can see that," Travis said dryly. "Who
taught you?"

"Rowdy."

Travis's glance swept down her body, starting at her
shoulders, moving past her waist, lingering on her
thighs and knees, before returning to her face. He
looked very unhappy, Rachel noted, but she wasn't
sure he was unhappy with her.

"Didn't Rowdy teach you how to sit a horse prop-
erly?" Travis asked.

Rachel blinked. "Sit a horse?" she repeated
dumbly.

"You know. You put your feet in the stirrups and
use your knees to keep your legs against the horse," he
explained impatiently. "That's it. Yeah, put 'em in.
Like this." He demonstrated, pressing his knees lightly
against his horse's belly. He smiled as she awkwardly
mimicked what he'd done. "Now, as you ride, move
with the horse in rhythm. Think of yourself as being
one with the horse, instead of bouncing along on top
of his back."

To Rachel's delight, his suggestions worked. Riding that way was infinitely more comfortable. And since she no longer had the feeling she was going to tumble off at any given moment, it wasn't as frightening to her, either. "Thanks," she said with a relieved sigh, knowing he hadn't had to help her, but had done so out of the goodness of his heart.

"Now, about the reins," Travis continued, ignoring her demonstrated relief. "How come you're holding one in each hand?"

Rachel shrugged. "That's what Rowdy told me to do. He said this way if I want to turn right, I pull the right rein. If I want to turn left, I pull the left." She studied Travis, who was holding his reins in one hand, effortlessly maneuvering his horse.

"Well, that way will work," Travis allowed, "but it's for beginners."

Travis looked more competent, Rachel had to admit. But it also seemed to her he was splitting hairs. If both ways worked, why not let her use the easy way to get around? "I don't see the difference," Rachel said.

"There isn't any, unless you need one hand free to lasso a stray calf. 'Course—" he winked at her '—considering the way you lasso and the fact you can barely sit a horse..." He ducked as she swatted her hat at him and nearly lost her balance and seat in the bargain. "I guess there's not much chance of that."

Rachel plopped her hat back on her head and, grasping the saddle horn with one hand, grumbled,

"Okay. You might as well show me how to ride with my reins in one hand."

"The same as you do with one in each hand, only now you have one hand free."

"What happens if I want my horse to go left?"

"Then you bring the reins to the right side of the horse," he explained simply. "That will automatically tauten the reins on the left, and bring the horse's head around."

"And the horse will go in whatever direction you point its head," Rachel finished.

"Right." Travis grinned at her. "Let's try it."

For the next several minutes, they rode around the pasture they were in. Rachel was confused at first, because it was opposite from the way she had learned, but Travis was an excellent teacher.

"Well, it's not second nature yet, but you've definitely almost got the hang of it," Travis finally allowed after she had successfully completed several tricky maneuvers.

"Thanks for the lofty praise," she said dryly as they continued on in the direction they'd started.

His eyes glimmered. "No false praise on this ranch," he countered flatly. "You either earn it or you don't."

"Double thanks."

"'Course, if you're out here all summer, you'll probably be riding like a tourist by summer's end. And actually that's kind of fitting, since you do work as a travel agent," he teased.

Rachel thought about reaching over and swatting him, then decided it wasn't worth the effort.

"Exactly when is your leave of absence at the travel agency up, anyway?" he asked.

Rachel rode on, enjoying the bright blue sky overhead and the warmth of the fair summer morning. She kept her eyes on the thick green grass and said, "I didn't take a leave of absence." Travis's brow arched speculatively and Rachel continued, "They wouldn't give me one. So I resigned."

His mouth thinned. And yet, Rachel mused, the action did nothing to detract from the sheer sensuality of his mouth.

"That was quite a gamble, wasn't it?"

"Not really." Rachel smiled, enjoying the one-upmanship between them almost as much as she enjoyed running the ranch. "As I don't intend to fail."

"Yeah, well, supposing you do?" he pressed, his head twisted and his eyes remaining unswervingly on hers as he moved his horse a little ahead. "Then what?"

Rachel felt her heartbeat pick up as she struggled to keep pace with him. And there was a definite heat wave starting up her neck, moving into her face. "Then I start over, come fall," she said defiantly.

They reached the pasture where her new herd was quartered. Travis swung himself out of his saddle. Before she could react, he was reaching up to give her a hand down. "You don't seem very concerned about the prospect of being unemployed," he said as soon as he had her on the ground. His hands tightened around her waist. "Unless, of course, you're planning to use your situation to pressure my mother into letting you and the twins stay on no matter what."

Rachel slipped out of his light grasp and tried not to think about how warm his hands had felt. Gentle, and yet resolute.

"I don't care what you think of me, Travis," she informed him as she had many times before. Turning her back on him, she strode over to the pasture fence and stared out at the scrawny-looking herd of Brahma calves. Most were about the size of large dogs, weighing no more than fifty pounds. It would be a year or more before they were ready to send to market. "I know, had it been up to him, that Austin would've wanted his children to share in his heritage," Rachel continued.

"Austin isn't here any longer," Travis pointed out as he positioned himself next to her.

"No, he isn't, but I still owe him. And this time, I'm not going to let him down," Rachel said grimly.

"This time? What do you mean this time?" Travis reached over and caught her arm.

"Nothing," Rachel said, ducking her head. She wasn't about to get into any of this with him. Not now. Maybe not ever.

"Rachel. You can't just leave it at—" Travis broke off abruptly as a low-flying helicopter swooped in overhead. It was white and had a red cross on the side.

And it seemed to be headed for a landing on Westcott land.

Suddenly Travis was all action. "Come on. Someone must've been hurt."

Minutes later, they were at the site of the commotion. "What happened?" Travis asked, jumping off his horse.

Rowdy wiped the sweat from his brow and pointed to a half-grown steer trussed up in a corner of the field. "Damned cow attacked one of my men."

Heart pounding, Rachel led the way to the stretcher, with Travis and Rowdy close on her heels. Rachel recognized the injured as being one of the newest hired hands, Bobby Ray Johnson.

She hunkered down beside him while the paramedics worked to immobilize his left shoulder and arm. "What happened?"

"I was out here working on the fence," Bobby Ray said weakly as the paramedic put the finishing touches on an air splint.

"You were working on it while the cows were in the field?" Rachel asked.

A shadow fell over her. "We always do that," Rowdy intervened.

"It's usually not a problem, Rachel," Travis said. "The pounding scares them off. They usually give us wide berth."

Concerned, Rachel turned back to Bobby Ray. "Did the cows leave you alone?"

"At first," Bobby Ray admitted. "Then I don't know what happened. I was just hammering the last new board when that crazy cow came up behind me and nudged me into the post. I turned around and gave him a hard slap on the side and yelled at him to get away, like I always do when one of 'em misbehaves or gets to crowding me. And that was when he charged me. If Rowdy hadn't been out here..." Bobby Ray shuddered, then grimaced in renewed pain. "I swear, Ms. Westcott, that cow's dangerous! I thought he was going to kill me!"

"I say we get rid of it," Rowdy said as soon as the helicopter had taken off with Bobby Ray toward the hospital in San Angelo.

Rachel strode toward the cow. Like all the cows on the ranch he had an ear tag that identified him by number for their records. His read #2021. At the moment, with his feet tied together, lying quietly on his side, the half-grown steer wasn't a danger to anyone. In fact, she thought, as she looked down into the big black eyes, he looked perfectly harmless. But appearances could be deceiving. "Has anyone called the vet?" she asked over her shoulder.

"Not yet," Rowdy said.

"Fine. I'll do that. Rowdy," Rachel directed, "you get this steer in quarantine in one of the pens next to the barn."

Rowdy touched a hand to the brim of his hat. "Yes, ma'am."

Travis followed Rachel to the pickup. He stuck his hands into the back pockets of his form-fitting jeans. "Mind filling me in on what you're doing?"

She shot him an impatient look. "I'm going to get Doc Harvey out here right away and have him take a look at that steer."

"What for?"

"To see if he's sick."

Travis shook his head disagreeably, their earlier camaraderie forgotten. "I can tell you right now that cow wasn't rabid."

"I wasn't necessarily thinking of rabies. He may have eaten some potato weed or western horse nettle—"

"Then the cow would've been acting drunk," Travis cut in, exasperated, "not mean."

"Unless he's a mean drunk," she corrected. She whirled to face him, wishing she could recapture the spirit of cooperativeness they had enjoyed earlier. "Look, we don't know what's going on with that cow," she said as she attempted to reason with him. "For all we know he could be sick with some contagious disease. But one thing is certain," she said firmly, refusing to let Travis's expertise sway her. "I am not going to make any decision on what to do with him until I have all the facts."

"ANY WORD ON BOBBY RAY?" Travis asked hours later as an exhausted Rachel walked in the back door to the ranch-house kitchen.

"He's resting comfortably at the hospital and due to be released tomorrow. He has a broken arm and a dislocated shoulder, though, so it'll be at least three months before he can work again at full speed."

"And in the meantime?" Travis asked, pouring Rachel a glass of lemonade.

She accepted the cold drink with thanks. "I told him we'd give him two weeks' paid sick leave and then he can come back to work on lighter chores after that."

"What about the cow?"

"Doc Harvey examined him and found no evidence that the cow had been into anything poisonous. Nor is #2021 sick."

Travis frowned. "I was afraid that would be the case."

To set Travis's mind at ease, Rachel told him her plans. "I'm going to continue to keep him under quarantine for another week or so."

"Why not just get rid of him now?" Travis persisted.

"Because he's only half-grown."

"You heard Bobby Ray. He thinks the animal's crazy."

Rachel set her glass down on the table with a thud. "Doc Harvey disagrees."

Wordlessly Travis reached into the drawer where the clean kitchen cloths were stored. He pulled out a tea towel and held it under the cool water. Then he wrung out the excess water and handed it wordlessly to Rachel, who rubbed it over her flushed face and neck.

"Look, I like Doc Harvey," Travis continued, propelling Rachel into the nearest chair, "but let's face it. He didn't grow up on a ranch and he hasn't been out of vet school all that long. He's still wet behind the ears when it comes to something like this."

"So is Bobby Ray, for that matter," Rachel countered calmly. She slouched down, propped up her feet on the seat of another chair and let her head fall back until it rested against the top rung. "So am I. What's your point?"

Travis stood with his legs braced apart and crossed his arms. "I really think you should get rid of the cow."

Rachel tore her eyes from his powerful frame and set her jaw stubbornly. She would not think about what being so close to him, so often, did to her. Or about how kind and thoughtful he could be when he was not trying to provoke her or actively get her off the ranch. "In another six months, that cow will be worth twice as much," she argued.

"In six months someone else could be hurt. Listen to me, Rachel." Travis's voice dropped a compelling notch. He dropped into the chair beside her, so that they were sitting face-to-face. "I've been around animals all my life. They're not that different from people. They've got personalities, too, and some of them are just plain mean."

Rachel lifted the heavy length of her hair off her neck. "Schizophrenic?"

"Yes."

Her feet hit the floor with a bang. She pushed away from the table, away from the by-now achingly familiar scent of his cologne. "That's an old wives' tale, Travis." She resented the fact he was so close, so concerned. And always, always underfoot!

"If someone else gets hurt..." he warned, coming around grimly to face her.

"It'll be on my conscience," Rachel said, tilting her head back and pulling in a deep breath. "But it's not going to happen, Travis."

Just as a real friendship between them probably wasn't going to happen. Despite his surface civility now, prompted by their mutual concern over the ranch and the safety of the men, she knew he didn't trust her any further than he could see her. And that, unfortunately, might never change, no matter what she said or did.

Chapter Six

"You've been awfully quiet this evening, Rachel," Jaclyn observed as the dessert dishes were being cleared away. "Any particular reason?"

Travis had been wondering the same thing. Used to Rachel's vivacity, he'd found her silence vaguely disturbing, too.

"I just can't believe that steer attacked Bobby Ray. Number 2021."

Jaclyn set down her coffee in alarm. "You haven't had any more trouble with him, have you?"

"No, but I think I'll go down and check on him, anyway, if you don't mind."

"Certainly you're excused," Jaclyn said graciously.

Travis stood up, too. "I'll go with you." He ignored the flash of dismay on her face. "I'm curious about how he's doing, too."

No sooner had the two of them left the dining room than Rachel extricated herself, rather pointedly, Travis thought, from his light guiding grasp.

"This really isn't necessary," she said through stiff lips.

He paused to get a flashlight from the shelf above the back door, and as he did so he took in the new style of her hair. She'd done something different tonight. Instead of wearing it loose, she'd pulled it off her neck and twisted it into an elegant figure eight. White and jade-green silk ribbons were threaded through it. He wasn't sure how she'd done it—it seemed complicated as all hell to him—but he liked it. It really looked elegant. And the pearl earrings she was wearing were another nice touch; they drew attention to the delicate lines of her face and made her seem all the more feminine.

"Save it. I'm going," Travis said. He glanced down at her slender legs and the two-inch heels that encased her feet. The jade-green pumps were perfect for showing off her slim legs during a semiformal dinner at home. Not so good for walking out in the yard. He sighed impatiently. "I'll wait while you put on a pair of boots."

"These shoes are fine," Rachel retorted.

"Suit yourself." Travis thrust an arm in front of her and held open the back door. "It's your ankle you'll be spraining."

"Don't you wish."

Travis could tell by the contentious gleam in her eyes that she was spoiling for another fight about what she'd done, or neglected to do, about the crazy cow. Feeling his own temper rise, he followed her to the corral. Unlike the yard surrounding the house, the corral was shadowed by the barns. The darkness was as soothing as the chirp of the cicadas in the trees, but there was enough moonlight for him to see even the slightest change in her face.

Her back to him, Rachel moved around to the left, until she could see steer #2021, standing alone at the far side of the pen. "You see," she said in a low victorious voice. "He's fine now."

"Sure he's fine," Travis agreed. "While he's by himself, penned up and eating the best grain the ranch has to offer."

"There is no reason to destroy him."

Travis rested both elbows on the top of the corral fence. He wished Rachel would stop being so stubborn. "We weren't talking about destroying him," he corrected. "We were talking about sending him off to be slaughtered, which I might point out, is going to happen sooner or later, anyway."

"He'll bring more money when he's fully grown."

Travis studied her, seeing a new way to tease her. "Are you sure you have what it takes to be a rancher? You're not going to cry when it comes time to slaughter the beef you're raising?"

Rachel tossed her head and looked down her nose at him. "No, I am not going to cry. I am well aware that ranching is a business, Travis. Which is exactly why I refused to let that cow go until he is grown and we can get a full return on our investment."

''You're right,'' Travis drawled provokingly. ''There is no reason to get rid of him now, except of course for the fact that he attacked one of our hands without provocation.''

Rachel's expression softened sympathetically, and for a moment she forgot to be angry with him. ''I'm sorry about what happened to Bobby Ray.'' One hand gripping the top rail, she leaned toward him earnestly. ''But I can't help but think there must have been a reason for what happened. Maybe the vet was wrong. Maybe Number 2021 did ingest some minute amount of potato weed that didn't show up in the tests. Maybe something *made* him act crazy.''

Travis raised a skeptical brow.

Rachel finished stonily, ''All I know is that cows, like people, deserve a second chance.''

''Are we talking about the cow now or you?'' he wondered aloud, knowing full well his question was likely to annoy her. Still, he wanted her to say literally everything that was on her mind, and if the only way to get her to do so was to provoke her, then so be it.

''Maybe a little of both.''

He studied her, watching the moonlight play on her hair. She looked guilty and upset. And so vulnerable he was tempted to forget the havoc she'd once caused his family and start fresh with her. ''What did you ever do wrong?'' he asked, curious about what she would admit to in her current frame of mind.

Shoulders slumping slightly, she moved away from him and stared out into the starry Texas night. ''You remember the day you came to tell us your father was disinheriting Austin?"

"Yes, I do." In fact, he remembered that day as if it was yesterday. He'd gone to their trailer early one morning, so early he'd gotten his brother and Rachel out of bed. She'd looked gorgeous, wrapped in a robe, her glorious red hair all tousled, her skin flushed with the warm glow of sleep. Austin had looked happy, too, despite the dismal poverty of their surroundings. Travis had felt guilty about being there, about doing his father's dirty work, yet he'd known, for his brother's sake, that Austin had to be told what their father was up to. Travis had delivered the blow. Rachel had left the room crying. Austin had cussed him and thrown him out. . . .

Rachel sighed now, and stared down at her clasped hands. "I was so sure that we were doing the right thing by staying married, Travis," she reported sadly. "I was so sure that we didn't need money and that we could be happy without it."

Seeing his brother and his new wife together for the first time, Travis had thought so, too. At least until he'd delivered the news.

"How did Austin feel?" Travis asked, wishing everything had been different, that the rift in his family hadn't occurred. And that Rachel and Austin had been given a chance to make it on their own without Westcott family interference.

Rachel shrugged listlessly, and when she spoke her voice sounded thick and unsteady, as if her throat was clogged with tears. "He tried to act like it didn't matter, but he was devastated, not just by Zeke's rejection of me, but of him, too. Oh, Travis," she said, blinking furiously, "he wanted to come back to the ranch so badly."

At that moment it was all Travis could do not to take Rachel into his arms and offer her the comfort he ached to give. "Why didn't he?"

"Pride. He knew if he brought me, Zeke would toss him out, and he wouldn't go without me."

"So he was stuck."

Rachel nodded affirmatively. Her voice gathered strength. "I tried to comfort him. But when weeks passed and he only got more depressed, I knew he'd never be happy without his family and his home. I couldn't take that away from him. Because I was standing in the way of any reconciliation, I did what I knew I had to do. I packed my bags and I told him it was over, that the marriage had been a mistake from the beginning, and I left."

Travis saw the sacrifice. It hadn't come easily to her. It hadn't been a whim, but a deliberate action, calculated to help his brother, not hurt and betray him. He studied her, realizing she was a much more complicated woman than he had ever given her credit for being. A much more compassionate woman. "Did he ever try to contact you after that?" He studied her upturned face.

"Yes." Rachel dropped her head forward. She rubbed at her temples with the fingertips of both hands. "I was very cruel, but I knew I had to be." She shook her head in obvious regret, shut her eyes and swallowed hard. "I didn't want him yearning after what could never be."

"And my mother?" Travis regarded Rachel sternly, telling himself not to let her beauty mislead him. He couldn't let himself forget that Rachel had taken money from his mother in the past, just as she was trying to take the ranch from Jaclyn, and from him, now. "How does my mother figure into this?"

Her arms hugging her chest, Rachel began to pace. "I don't know how she found me. Maybe Austin told her where I'd gone. But I got a letter from her, telling me how sorry she was things had worked out the way they had, and she praised me for doing what I felt I had to. I think she knew what it was costing me to give Austin up. At the time, he was all I had.

"Anyway—" she ducked her head, embarrassed "—there was a check enclosed, to help me make a fresh start. A week later, Austin was dead. And all I had," she said softly, "were my regrets."

"You didn't come to the funeral," Travis accused, remembering how stunned and hurt he'd been about that.

"I couldn't," she said sadly. "I didn't want to upset Zeke."

She'd been right, Travis thought. Her coming to the funeral would have made his father crazy with rage and hurt.

"But later," Rachel continued, "I visited Austin's grave and said goodbye in my own way."

Travis wanted to believe she had loved his brother and wanted only what was best for him. Still, there was much he had to ask, much he had to examine about her character. "If Austin hadn't died," he said slowly, "would you and he have gotten back together because of the twins?" He discovered, to his surprise, that he wanted her to say no as much as he wanted her to say yes. It was painful for him to think of her with Austin, and yet painful for him to think of her hurting Austin, too.

Rachel shrugged again. "That I just can't say, Travis," she said, her chin lifting a defiant notch.

He admired her honesty. "Why didn't you ever tell me any of this?" Why hadn't she just leveled with him from day one?

"Because you weren't ready to listen."

Travis almost ducked his head in shame. He knew that was true. He also knew his feelings had changed in the weeks she'd been on the ranch. Initially, he had wanted nothing more than to make her leave. But that was before he had started to get to know her. Now, that wasn't what he wanted at all. He still didn't want her running the ranch, though. He never would. The ranch was his rightful inheritance, not hers. And yet the thought of her leaving, of rarely if ever seeing her again, bothered him more than he wanted to admit.

She glanced over her shoulder. "They'll be wondering what's keeping us."

Yes, Travis thought, they certainly would.

"We better go back in."

"Look, Miz Westcott, I've been talking to the men and we're all in agreement. We want that crazy cow to go."

Rachel squared off with Rowdy in the bunkhouse while the men listened. "If the cow were still acting up, I'd be tempted to agree with you, but he's not."

"He wasn't acting up before he attacked me, either," Bobby Ray said from his place at one of the long plank tables.

Guilt pushed at Rachel as she recalled Bobby Ray in the back of the helicopter. Even now, he would be weeks recovering. "I'm sorry about what happened to you, Bobby Ray. But I've talked to Doc Harvey—"

"Who just happens to be as green as a kid fresh out of high school," Rowdy harrumphed.

"That's enough, Rowdy," Rachel said tightly. "Doc Harvey is extremely well qualified and you know it."

"Going to school doesn't mean he knows anything about range work," Rowdy spat back. "And I know that crazy cow's mama. She was as mean as her calf is now. Ornery and ill-tempered."

Rachel faced Rowdy stubbornly. She was so tired of him challenging her. Worse, she knew the rest of the men took their cues from their foreman. If she couldn't get him on her side, or at least make him respect her, she would never be able to run the Bar W smoothly. Making no effort to conceal the exaspera-

tion in her voice, she volleyed back, "We're not looking for Mr. Congeniality, Rowdy, just a full-grown
steer to take to market."

Rowdy shot her a challenging look. "I still say we
get rid of him."

"When it's time," Rachel qualified. "Now, we'll
continue to keep the cow isolated and under observa-
tion."

"And if there's any more trouble?" Bobby Ray
challenged, looking just a bit fearful.

"Then I'll make a decision at that time," Rachel
said gently, surer than ever she was doing the right
thing in refusing to let either of the men, or one
slightly crazy cow, intimidate her. "Now, about the
pesticide-free feed for the organically raised herd. I
noticed we're getting a little low." She glanced at
Rowdy. "Have you ordered more?"

"Not yet. I think they're ripping us off, price-wise.
I was looking around for a cheaper supplier."

"Keep trying to find one. In the meantime, order
another week's supply of pesticide-free grain from the
current source."

"It costs double the ordinary grain," Rowdy protested.

"I'm aware of that," Rachel said quietly. "But if we
feed them anything else the herd won't be organically
raised. And then it will all have been for naught, won't
it?"

Rowdy met her stare for stare. "Suit yourself," he said. He turned and headed for his adjacent office. "It's the Westcott's money."

And not mine, Rachel supposed he meant.

Realizing the gauntlet had been thrown down and that all the men were watching for her reaction Rachel said, with deadly calm, "Rowdy, I understand things are being run differently now. If you're having trouble doing the job..." She left the words hanging, but the threat in her voice was implicit. And real.

Jaw set, he whirled back to face her. "I can do the job," he retorted tersely. His eyes, full of resentment, bore into hers.

Too late, Rachel realized she had made a mistake by crossing him in front of the men. She had a brief uneasy feeling her cow boss was going to extract some sort of revenge for this public dressing-down.

"Fine," she said.

Rowdy's chest rose and fell with the effort it was taking to control his temper. He removed his hat and slapped it against his thigh. "About the mesquite in pasture forty-one. What do you want us to do about that?"

TRAVIS WAS IN HIS OFFICE when Rachel found him. Observing his tall frame in the converted sewing room, Rachel felt another pang of guilt. The heavy furniture from his father's office had been crammed into a room that was barely a quarter the size. Computer listings and manila files were stacked on every available surface. His computer, fax, copier, phone and answering machine covered the rest. Travis barely had room for the swivel chair behind the desk. Worse, the Cape Cod curtains and sunshine-yellow color scheme added a ludicrously frilly touch to what should have been a businesslike domain.

But he didn't have to work here, she reminded herself sternly when her guilt threatened to get the better of her. He had an undoubtedly spacious office in Fort Worth. She did have to work here. She wouldn't waste any time worrying about a situation he had created for himself. She had enough to do just trying to solve the problems on the ranch.

Rachel rapped on the door frame. "Got a minute?" she asked casually.

Travis leaned back in his father's old swivel chair. His black hair mussed, his eyes clear and vibrantly alive, he looked handsome, self-assured, and very male. He tossed the computer printout he'd been studying onto a pile of papers on his cluttered desk. "What's up?"

Rachel tore her eyes from the long legs propped on one corner of the desk and the way his jeans fit those legs snugly from the top of his boots to his waist, and every point in between. She lounged against the door frame. "Rowdy and some of the other hands want me to cut down the mesquite in pasture forty-one. I know they hog water and the grass there is drying out, but the trees also provide shade. I'm hesitant to take away what little relief from the heat the cattle have."

"Yeah, so?" He leaned farther back in his chair.

"So..." Rachel took a deep breath, put aside her considerable pride and prepared to ask for help. "I'm wondering what you would do if you were in my place."

Travis's eyes stayed on hers a reflective moment.

She felt the jolt of his intent assessing look all the way down to her toes. Like an ongoing electrical current, it had every inch of her thrumming and alive.

His sexy smile widened to a taunting depth. "Ah, but Rachel, I'm not in your place, remember?" he reminded her lazily. His gaze roved her face with contemplative pleasure. "My mother and you saw to that."

Rachel fought the heat creeping up her neck and the urge to throttle him. Damn him, she thought, for enjoying every second of her discomfiture. Her voice choking with suppressed indignation, she surmised grimly, "You're not going to give me any advice, are you?"

He took his clasped hands, lifted them high above his head, stretched every muscle in his brawny arms and chest, then moved them to the back of his neck. His eyes on hers, he tipped his chair back even farther. "It'd kind of spoil the fun if I told you what to do, wouldn't it?" he taunted in a soft provoking voice that sent shivers up and down her spine. He studied her intently, then shrugged. "You're running the ranch now. You decide."

So much for expecting him to be decent, kind, caring or helpful in any way. She swore and turned smartly on her heel. "You're a selfish bastard."

His laughter was low and enticing, and it filled the sewing room to overflowing. Then he made a *tsking* sound. "Rachel, Rachel. I'm surprised at your language."

Rachel kept going and didn't look back. The only surprise she had was her own stupidity for expecting him to help her in the first place. Just because he'd been nice to her once the other night, just because they'd actually had one civil adult conversation and he had seemed to come away from it with a better understanding of what she'd been through with his brother, didn't alter anything. He still wanted her off the ranch. And no matter how tense, unhappy or unwelcome that made her feel, she reflected sorrowfully, his attitude wasn't going to change.

Chapter Seven

"Where the devil have you been?" Travis asked hours later when Rachel strode into the house, her red cowboy boots clicking authoritatively on the tile floor. "Dinner was over an hour ago."

Rachel was still stinging from the way he had dismissed her request for advice, but her pride compelled her not to let him know it. All too aware that his eyes assessed every inch of her, she shoved her dust-covered, flat-brimmed hat off her head and let it fall down her back, held around her neck by the long leather string. "Careful, cowboy, you're beginning to sound like you actually care about me."

He watched her wipe the sweat from her face with her sleeve. His expression was grim. "That's not funny."

"Neither was missing dinner," Rachel retorted. She deeply inhaled the scents of freshly baked bread and mesquite-smoked turkey. "And it smells like it was delicious." Turning to the Westcott's cook, Maria, she said, "I have to eat on the run tonight, so would you mind fixing me a couple of sandwiches and a thermos of iced tea?''

"It's no problem, Rachel," Maria said. "I'd be happy to do it. And I'll put in some fruit and cookies for you, too." Maria moved off, her bulky figure bustling into action.

"You still haven't answered my question," Travis prodded. "Where have you been?"

Her glance trailed down his tall form. Instead of the usual coat and tie he wore for dinner, he, too, was dressed in jeans. "You're not exactly dressed for dinner, either."

"I was."

"And?"

"And what?"

Rachel tore her eyes from the crisp dark hair curling out of the open V of his collar. "And where are *you* going now?"

"I *was* going out to look for you. Which brings me back to my original question," he countered. "What's going on? Where've you been?"

Pointedly ignoring his request for further information the way he had ignored her plea for help earlier, she turned to Maria. "Give my apologies to Jaclyn and the children and tell them I'll be back in a few hours."

"Wait a minute," Travis said. He followed her as she picked up the paper bag containing her food and a box of garden tools, then strode out the back door and into the driveway. "Where are you going?"

"Where does it look like?" Rachel tossed the words dryly over her shoulder. "Back out to the range."

"To do what?"

Rachel stood on tiptoe and put the tools into the bed of the pickup. "Wouldn't you like to know?" she shot back almost flirtatiously.

"Believe it or not—" he stepped in front of her, blocking her way "—that is why I asked."

Rachel elbowed him aside and yanked open the door of the driver's side. "Well, forgive me if I don't see any reason I should tell you."

He watched as Rachel tossed her lunch in, then climbed into the pickup and slid behind the wheel.

He slammed the door shut for her and leaned in through the open window. "I'm trying to be helpful," he explained patiently.

"You were anything but helpful this morning." Rachel tried to shove the key into the ignition, frowned when she realized it wasn't the right one and put in another, wiggling it until it fit.

"That was different," Travis countered defensively.

Rachel turned her head and sent him a long cold look. "Why?"

He leaned in closer. His smile was mischievous and provoking. "*That* involved basic decision making. *This* involves tools."

"Chauvinist." She turned the ignition key, floored the accelerator and gunned the engine.

He cut around the front and hopped into the passenger side before she could stop him. "Now that we've established that, how about letting me drive?"

"Forget it!"

"That's what I thought," he sighed. "So where are *we* going?" he asked.

"Back out to pasture fifty-three!"

"What's happening there?"

Rachel adjusted the rearview mirror and tried not to notice how the alluring scent of him filled the cab. "Broken windmill."

"Why don't you have one of the hands look at it?"

"Because they're all out thinning the mesquite by half in pasture forty-one right now. Besides," she continued confidently, "I figured I could do it myself."

His eyes roved her face, her shoulders, her arms, her hands, before returning with laser accuracy to her eyes. "What do you know about windmills?"

"Nothing," Rachel responded blithely, infuriated that for some strange reason she couldn't seem to take anything but shallow breaths. Maybe it was the lack of food, combined with the heat, doing her in. Certainly, she thought, it had nothing to do with him! Holding the wheel with one hand, she rummaged with her right into the sack. The truck hit a rut and lurched hard to the right. "Now what are you doing?" he asked.

Rachel grimaced and put both hands on the wheel again. "Trying to get a sandwich out for myself. Guess dinner will have to wait."

The truck hit another rut.

Travis swore as his elbow collided with the passenger door. "If you'd let me drive—"

"What? And let it be said I'm leaning on you?" She laughed bitterly and kept her eyes on the road. "No thanks, cowboy."

"Rachel, you don't have to carry it this far," he advised with brotherly exasperation.

"The heck I don't!" She turned the truck into the entrance to pasture fifty-three and jerked it to a halt just short of the motionless windmill. She cut the engine and ticked off her list of grievances. "Every time I turn around, my authority is being questioned. You're letting me know, one way or another, I don't belong here. Rowdy and the men are doing the same thing."

Travis's eyes narrowed. "Rowdy's still giving you a hard time?"

"Careful, you're beginning to sound protective, and we wouldn't want that, would we?" She slammed out of the truck, not knowing why she was so upset. Only that every time she was around him she was tense and on edge, expectant almost, as if she was waiting, no wanting, something to happen, the way it had that night in her office when he'd kissed her.

Travis got out quietly. He picked up her food sack, closed the door firmly and strode to her side. "Is Rowdy still giving you a hard time?" he repeated.

Rachel shrugged, sorry she'd said anything. "No more than you. Forget I said anything, okay?"

He handed her the sack. Though she'd been incredibly hungry just moments before, she found her appetite was all but gone now. Nonetheless, she sat down on the front bumper of the truck, pulled out a sandwich and began to eat.

When she'd finished, she joined Travis in inspecting the windmill. "I noticed right away what the trouble was," she said, between gulps of iced tea. "Weeds have grown up and around the wheel. I think once I cut through that garbage and clean it out, it'll start turning again and we'll get some water moving from the irrigation pond into the creek bed."

"How long has it been this way?" Travis asked with a disapproving frown.

Rachel shrugged, feeling pleased that he seemed to agree with her assessment of the situation. "I'm not sure. We haven't had any cattle out here since the first week I was on the ranch." She capped her thermos and headed back to the pickup for the tools, her strides long and purposeful. "But we're fixing to move some out tomorrow morning, so it's got to be fixed before then."

She cast a dubious glance at the falling sun. It slid, a bright red ball, toward the crimson-and-pink horizon. She tried not to worry. "Hopefully I've got enough daylight," she said when she returned to Travis's side.

It was still hotter than blazes. Sweat dotted her forehead. Figuring her hat would get in the way more than it would help, she took it off. Taking the bandanna from her neck, she tied it around her forehead and caught the ends of her hair in a coated elastic band. Travis began to pace as she surveyed her tools. "Something bothering you?" she asked.

"Like what?" he challenged.

"I don't know. You've got a funny look on your face." *As if you want to help me out and you don't.*

Wordlessly he followed her down to the base of the windmill. Dropping to his haunches, he examined the tangled undergrowth in the thick wooden cog more closely. "Is that supposed to be a compliment?"

"Take it however you want," Rachel said as she hopped down into the empty dirt-and-gravel-lined canal where the water should have been flowing.

"You know..." Travis began thoughtfully as she started to hack away at the undergrowth with a pair of shears.

"What?"

"Never mind." He stalked away. Rachel shot a glance at his retreating back, so broad and masculine, then turned her attention to the task. There wasn't much daylight left, she warned herself sternly. She couldn't afford to dally, never mind concentrate on his sexy loose-boned walk. Besides, if she fixed this windmill by herself, it would improve her standing with the men. After her last blowup with Rowdy, she needed every bit of credibility she could get. Above her, Travis had resumed his pacing to distracting effect.

Suddenly Travis's shadow was looming over her, blocking out the dwindling sun. "I'm surprised at your expertise," he commented as she dug out a handful of thick reeds and tossed them up on the bank beside her with a gloved hand.

"You're telling me you couldn't easily do the same?" she returned lightly.

"No. As it happens, there isn't a job on this ranch I couldn't, or maybe I should say haven't done." He jumped down into the empty irrigation ditch beside her.

"Wait a minute." She planted a dusty glove in the center of his chest and held him away from the wheel. "I thought I told you I wanted to do this alone."

"So you said," Travis retorted, "but I'm tired of standing around."

Rachel told herself her sudden breathlessness was from the exertion, nothing else.

"If you're worried about anyone finding out," Travis bartered, "we won't tell them I gave you a hand, okay?"

Rachel continued to hold him off, the flat of her hand against his hard flexed muscles. Beneath her palm, she could feel the strong quick beat of his heart. "Why are you being so nice?" she asked.

"Because it's damned hard not to be. I was raised to always help a lady," he explained tersely, sounding irritated with himself.

She arched a brow and sent him a disbelieving look. "Could've fooled me lately," she drawled.

"Yeah, well, your taking over the ranch is different," he growled. His hand swung up to catch her wrist. His grip light but firm, he forced her hand down between them, held it one long breath-stealing moment, then let it go.

Rachel ignored the frantic beating of her heart. "Because the ranch is territory?"

"And then some," he agreed.

"And we all know how males are about their territory," she baited.

"Of any kind."

She shook her head at him. He wasn't talking about anything specific. It was her fault she was thinking about *romantic* territory, and how fiercely Travis would guard a woman he considered his. "So why are you suddenly being so nice?"

He reached behind her for a scythe. "I'm not doing it for you. I'm doing it for the cattle."

"Right," she said wryly.

He crouched down beside her and began hacking at the lowermost tangle of plants. Three strokes and he'd completely cleared one cog of the big wooden wheel. Rachel watched, amazed at his physical expertise. "You've done this before," she guessed.

"As it happens, plenty of times." He stood and pointed to a cog at the top. "Your turn."

Aware her own motions were much less powerful than his, Rachel began cutting through the growth. "I always thought you were more an executive, a manager," she commented, reasoning that idle talk would make their job go faster.

"At my airlines, yeah. Here at the ranch, though, I've always been an able hand." He grunted with the force behind his swings of the scythe. His mouth compressed grimly. "My dad saw to that."

Rachel marveled that his mouth could look so sensual and appealing even when he was frowning. "What do you mean?"

Travis continued to hack away rhythmically while she snipped and tugged with equal ferocity. "Dad didn't want either of his sons turning into sissified city slickers," Travis confided. "So from the time we were old enough to walk he kept us busy doing all the dirtiest jobs on the ranch. He made us learn the ranch from the bottom up, and even so—" Travis's voice faded "—I had the feeling, in Dad's eyes, that neither of us ever *quite* measured up."

Rachel heard the hurt in Travis's voice. She, too, knew what it was like to have a less than satisfactory relationship with a parent. Angry at Zeke for what he'd put them all through, she tore out another handful of weeds. "Your dad was pretty rough on both you guys, wasn't he?"

Travis nodded. "More so Austin than me, though." He exhaled and continued reflectively, "I'm not sure if it was just because Austin was the oldest, or because he planned from the beginning for Austin to take over the ranch, but Dad was on Austin's back constantly." Travis shook his head.

"But you?"

Travis shrugged his powerful shoulders. "He prodded me, too, incessantly I sometimes felt, but it was never as bad for me, because I was the second son and hence less important in my Dad's eyes. Or... I don't know. Maybe it was just because he spent so much time trying to make Austin grow up right that he didn't have as much time for me."

Rachel tore her eyes from the trim fit of his jeans. "I know how being second feels. It's not a good feeling."

"But you were an only child," Travis protested, turning toward her.

"And second-best to my daddy's gin." She sat back on her heels, her chest heaving with exertion. Their eyes met in a moment of understanding. "It's hard when, for whatever reason, you don't quite measure up in your parent's eyes."

"And harder still when your parent lets you down," Travis added with a stern look, letting her know he considered her father's drinking to be her father's problem and not hers.

Rachel went back to the few weeds that were left. Travis tossed his scythe aside. With a tremendous creak and a groan, the huge wheel began to turn. And once it had started to move, there was no holding anything back. Water came rushing out, splashing down, the sheer force of it sending them back against the bank. Knocked off balance, Rachel slipped and would have fallen had Travis's strong arm not anchored around her waist. He pulled her swiftly against him and held her there, the strength in his powerful body an easy match for the force of rushing water.

One hand beneath her hip, he shoved her up and toward the bank. "Climb on out," he said above the noise of the wheel and the water.

She did as directed, water streaming out of her pants and down her legs. He followed shortly thereafter, looking as wet and uncomfortable as she was. "Are you okay?" he asked.

Rachel nodded, but her legs had the consistency of putty. Wordlessly he slid his arm about her waist and held her against him. He got her steadied again, but his eyes never left hers. Before she knew what was happening, his mouth was covering hers, bringing with it the salty taste of his skin and the fragrant scent of his cologne, and then the whole world exploded in myriad sensations. She was aware of so many things. The heat of the warm summer night and the greater heat of his body. The descending darkness. The rock solidness of his chest teasing the growing tightness of her breasts. The strength of his thighs, the burgeoning proof of his desire.

Most of all, she was aware of his kiss. It was hot and delicious and steaming with the prospect of so much more. There was something inevitable between them, something she no longer seemed to have the strength or will to fight. She went limp as a rag doll as his tongue entered her mouth and swept the insides with luxurious abandon. She sighed when he brought her tongue into play with his. And she arched against him when he withdrew his tongue, only to coax her lips apart and slide it inside her mouth once again. Over, around, inside, out. She wanted more of him, wanted more of this, she thought dizzily, as her fingertips threaded through the thatch of hair curling against his nape and her mouth clung to his with riveting abandon. She didn't care if it was crazy. It felt too good.

And still he kissed her, long and hard and deep. An ache started in her chest and drifted inexorably lower, to her middle, then lower still, to her thighs. His mastory was riveting, and far too wonderful to try to stop. Giving in to the moment completely, she angled her body up and into his, softness to hardness. The fierceness of his desire against her middle ignited her senses like a match to dry tinder. Gratification and desire combined and swept through her in compelling waves.

She hadn't known it could be like this. Hadn't guessed at her own reaction to him, but now that it was happening, she seemed powerless. She couldn't protest when he hooked his arms around her waist and lowered her slowly to the ground.

His body stretched out beside hers. "Hot damn, Rachel," he whispered almost prayerfully, raining kisses across her face before once again settling on her lips. "You're sweet . . . so good."

And he was, too, she thought, as his knee parted hers. Nimbly, he unbuttoned her blouse. His head dipped lower. His tongue lashed damp fire across the swell of her breasts. She held her breath in expectation as he unfastened the front clasp of her lacy bra and parted the edges. The warm summer air tickled her skin. He cupped her breast with the base of his hand, lifting the taut nipple, rubbing it tenderly with his thumb. She cried out as his mouth covered the aching crown and arched her back yet again as he increased the sweet pressure with his mouth, wanting completion.

Just when she thought she couldn't stand it any longer, he moved to her other breast and gave it the same loving treatment. "Travis," she whispered urgently, curling her hands into his hair.

"I know, sugar," he whispered as she squirmed impatiently beneath him. Lifting his head, he gazed down at her as if she were the most beautiful woman on earth. He slid over, so he was between her thighs.

Mindless with need, Rachel unsnapped his shirt and yanked the edges apart. His eyes still on hers, he reached for the snap of her jeans. She sucked in her breath as he slid the zipper down and slipped his hand inside. His mouth covered hers as his hand dipped even lower, diving through the soft downy curls to the apex of her thighs. Rachel whimpered helplessly as he found and stroked the most sensitive part of her. Again and again. Until every inch of her was on fire, aching for more.

Both hands on her hips, he slid her jeans lower. She helped him with the unfastening of his jeans. As her hands and eyes found him, she again sucked in her breath. And then there was no more time to think. He was kneeling over her, his hands beneath her hips. Lifting her. Sliding inside.

The impact of their joining was electric. Reveling in it, he went deep and held her tight. She clung to him as they kissed, a thousand conflicting emotions whirling inside her. Desire, despair, shame, hunger and wanton abandon. But most of all, she thought, as he began to move once again, slowly at first, then more and more confidently, she wanted this. Needed this. She needed, heaven help her, him.

"Travis..." Her hands curled into the muscled firmness of his back. "Oh, Travis. I...please..."

"Not yet," he murmured, as he slid a hand between them, stroking, lower and lower. Again, he found her. The last tiny vestiges of her restraint fled. She went tumbling over the edge, mind and body spinning. He joined her, and together they catapulted heedlessly toward oblivion.

Minutes—or was it hours or just seconds?—later, Rachel's breath had slowed. And it was then, only then, that her common sense returned. *Dear Lord, what had she done?*

Hand to his chest, Rachel shoved him off her and jerked from the warm tempting circle of his arms. It didn't matter that he kissed like no one else, that he made her feel as no one else ever had, not even Austin. It didn't matter that what they'd just shared had felt like love. She *knew* it wasn't.

She yanked her jeans up and struggled to her feet, swearing vituperatively all the while. Scalding tears stung her eyes. "I can't believe I just did that," she cried, yanking the edges of her blouse together.

Travis struggled to his feet, too. His shirt open, his jeans up but unzipped, he looked sexy, tousled, dazed at first and then dangerous. "I've heard of regrets," he drawled. "But isn't this a little soon?"

She wasn't in the mood for any of his lazy humor. "Shut up!" She aimed a killer blow at his chest.

He caught her wrist before it connected and yanked her against him, the action not exactly ungentle, but not one that could be resisted, either. "You're beautiful, you know that?" he whispered compellingly, raining soft tempting kisses down her face. "And I want you again."

At his touch, Rachel's insides turned to hot liquid. Her thighs turned to butter. But her resolve not to make the same mistake twice remained strong. "No," she said, stepping back as far as his grip on her would allow. She drew in a harsh panting breath. *"No!"*

Reluctantly he let go of her wrist, studied her silently. If he had any regrets at all, Rachel thought sourly as she observed him, he was hiding them well.

"Okay," he acceded finally. "Maybe it was a little fast."

"A little!" she echoed, incensed.

"It still happened," he insisted.

Rachel drove her hands through her hair, pushing it off her face. "Not again, Travis. We can't and won't do this ever again."

"Why the hell not?" He advanced on her. His hands rested on her shoulders, warm and compelling. "It was good for you. I know it was," he persisted softly, his eyes tenderly searching her face. "I felt your climax, Rachel." His voice dropped another seductive notch. "You were like a tight, hot glove, wrapped around me like wet velvet—"

She jerked away from him and put her hands over her ears, hating the vivid memories his words evoked almost as much as she hated herself for melting inside like a giddy teenager whenever she was near him. "Don't," she moaned. *Don't make me want you again!*

"Why not?" Hand in the waist of her jeans, he swung her around to face him. His other hand slid under her chin, forcing her head up. "Does it hurt that much for you to face the truth?" he whispered hoarsely, something suspiciously like hurt glimmering in his eyes. "To admit to me that we might actually want each other, be good for each other?"

She laughed bitterly. He was making this sound simple. And it wasn't. What they had shared was lust, plain and simple, not love. The depth of her shame sent heat into her cheeks as she remembered how wantonly, how irresponsibly, she had just behaved. Never had she done anything so foolish and short-sighted, so guaranteed to bring embarrassment and heartache. Maybe it was de rigueur for him, confirmed bachelor that he was, but it wasn't for her! Furiously she sputtered back, "The only thing our, uh..."

"Lovemaking?" he supplied dryly. His look hardened accusingly. "You can't even say it, can you?"

She took a deep breath, refusing to let him suck her into another pointless argument. Granted, what they had just done was reckless, but it didn't mean they had to continue acting that way. Drawing the lacy halves of cloth together, she reclasped the front of her bra. "Obviously our physical needs took precedent tonight," she said, forcing calm into her voice as she rebuttoned her shirt. "But it will never happen again, Travis. Never." She wouldn't let it.

"Why not?" he challenged, watching as she refastened her belt.

Rachel steadfastly avoided his eyes as she stared at the ground where they'd just made love. "Because there's too much at stake."

"Like what?" He towered over her. "The ranch?" he taunted softly, wickedly. "Or your own ambition and greed?"

"All that and my children's future," Rachel acknowledged with a regal nod, denying nothing because she wanted him to think the very worst of her.

"I won't risk their inheritance, Travis. Not for any man. And certainly not for another ill-advised roll in the hay with you!"

He stared at her as if seeing her for the very first time. "You're really cold-blooded, aren't you?" he ground out.

"Yes," Rachel lied, "I am." Knowing it was her best defense against his passion, she finished aloofly, "Remember that the next time you're tempted to do—" she inclined her head toward the ground where they had just lain "—that."

She turned on her heel and marched defiantly toward the pickup. As she walked away from him, Travis swore virulently through his teeth. But whatever he said about her—and he said plenty—couldn't begin to top what she was saying about herself. She had never felt lower in her life.

Chapter Eight

"Travis, I want to know what's going on," Jaclyn insisted over the long-distance phone line. "You haven't been home for three days now. Is there some problem with your airlines?"

"Just the usual overload of summer business, resultant equipment failures and rescheduling crises," Travis said dryly.

"Then why aren't you home?" Jaclyn persisted.

Because of Rachel and what happened between us the other night, Travis thought. He was still steamed by the way she had reacted after they'd made love. Like it was the crime of the century or something, instead of something that was . . . well, inevitable.

"The children, Brett in particular, both miss you," Jaclyn continued.

"They have you and Rachel," Travis argued gruffly.

"True, but it's not the same as having a man around the house, Travis, and Brett is at an age where he needs a male role model in his life."

Travis leaned back in his swivel chair. His secretary stood in the doorway, a sheaf of papers in her hands. Travis waved her in wordlessly and took the papers. He smiled his thanks before she retreated.

"How is everything at the ranch?" Travis asked, aware that he missed being there. He missed being at the heart of things. And he missed seeing Rachel. He'd never been so sexually attracted to a woman in his life. And it wasn't just that. He liked being with her, even when they were fighting. He liked seeing her get all feisty. He liked the fact that she was not only strong enough to do battle with him, but refused to back down, no matter what she felt the odds of her winning. He liked seeing her eyes light up with temper. And even better, he liked seeing them grow all misty and soft with desire....

"I'll tell you how it is around here. It's lonely," Jaclyn finally said.

Well, Travis thought, it wasn't his fault Rachel couldn't handle having a short-term love affair. If he were smart, he'd avoid her entirely. And yet how could he do that and still watch over his family's interests in the ranch?

"Rachel and I both want you home," Jaclyn continued.

Hope flared briefly, like a match in the dark. "She said that?" Travis asked, sitting forward. He rested his elbows on his desk and tried not to think about the heat that filled his lower body at just the thought of

Rachel. And how she'd felt against him, so soft and womanly, when they'd made love.

"No, but I know she's thinking it," Jaclyn replied.

Travis closed his eyes and let out a beleaguered breath. Much as he didn't want to, he could recall all too clearly the look in Rachel's eyes the last time he'd seen her. She'd been fiercely angry.

"Travis," his mother demanded impatiently. "Are you paying attention to anything I'm saying?"

Travis sighed. Normally he tried to help his mother, but in this instance she had no idea what she was asking of him. Especially when his brain was telling him he needed to forget about the passion that had flared between him and Rachel and stay on his original course. He'd give Rachel enough rope to hang herself, and she'd prove she was incompetent to run the Bar W.

Unfortunately he was having a hell of a time doing that. The gentler side of him wanted to encourage and help and protect her. The gentler side kept urging him to forget that she was out to steal his rightful inheritance.

"Look, Mom..." he began irritably, wishing he could tell his mother the truth. But he could hardly reveal how tempted he was by Rachel's beauty, her style, her gutsiness and temper and strength.

"Say you'll come to dinner tonight, Travis. Please."

His guilt at disappointing and hurting his mother held him motionless. Whether he wanted to admit it or not, he did have a responsibility to his family and to the ranch. And he couldn't keep running from his desire. The only way to deal with it was to face it, and then not act on it.

"All right," Travis promised reluctantly. "You've talked me into it. I'll be home for dinner tonight."

TWO HUNDRED AND FIFTY miles away, Rachel knelt in the searing noonday heat and surveyed the damage in pasture forty-nine. It was one of the best sources of grass and water they had, but almost overnight, it seemed, the pasture was full of holes and long mysterious furrows. "What's causing this?"

"Jackalopes," Rowdy said, surveying the yellowing summer grass. "Definitely jackalopes."

Rachel swore silently to herself. Great, she thought. Something else she didn't know about, and there was no use pretending she did. She straightened slowly and turned to face him, glad that her flat-brimmed hat shielded her face from both the scorching summer sun and him. "What's a jackalope?"

Rowdy kicked the toe of his boot into the opening of one of the shallow furrowlike burrows, approximately six feet in length. "It's kind of a cross between a prairie jackrabbit and a gopher. They burrow down to get away from the heat. When it's as hot as it has been, well, you can see how quickly they do damage." He kicked at the burrow again.

Rachel counted fifty or sixty such holes in the pasture. It was easy to see they were more than just a nuisance. A cow could easily turn an ankle or break a leg. "How do we get rid of them?"

Rowdy scowled. "Can't put out any poison. The cattle might get ahold of it."

"Of course."

"Only solution is traps. But you can't set 'em up in the daytime 'cause the jackalopes are smart enough to see them and run away. You have to do it at night." Frustrated, he strode back and forth, muttering a string of curses. "These are all over the ranch. It's going to take every man available and we'll still be short."

He turned to her. "In the heat, they burrow constantly, searching for water, cool earth. Another week this hot, without rain, and there's no telling the amount of damage they'll do to the ranch." A grim yet challenging look flared in his eyes. "I don't suppose you'd want to help?"

"Of course I'll help," Rachel said, wanting him and the men to know she wasn't above getting her hands dirty. "What kind of traps are we going to use?"

"EXACTLY HOW OFTEN is Rachel not showing up for dinner?" Travis asked his mother. It was nine-thirty. The twins had retired to the game room to watch a movie.

"She's been out on some ranch-related calamity or another all week," his mother confessed, pouring herself a cup of coffee from the silver service on the coffee table. "Frankly, I'm tempted to interfere. On the other hand, I did give her free rein. And now that the men are beginning to accept her as their boss, I fear if I try to step in and tell her to slow down that she might take it the wrong way."

"And assume you're telling her that because you think she's not capable?"

His mother nodded. "Exactly. I know how much she's had to struggle and study. I know how hard she's trying to prove herself. I only want to support her." Jaclyn sighed. "It means not interfering in how she chooses to run the family business, even if she is running herself into the ground to do it."

Travis frowned. He had never wanted Rachel to succeed at running the ranch and he still didn't but he didn't want her ruining her health, either. "What does Rowdy have to say about all this?"

"I don't know. I haven't seen much of him, either. Travis." Alarm colored her low tone as he strode toward the door. "Where are you going?"

"To see what's going on." He had a hunch something was. And whatever it was, it wasn't good for Rachel.

The lights were ablaze in the bunkhouse when Travis stepped outside the ranch house and started across the yard. A glance in the sprawling multivehicle garage showed that all but one of the ranch pickups were there. Which meant one of two things, he thought. Either Rachel wasn't sharing with the men whatever problem she was having and hence the men weren't helping her solve it, or she was up to something else.

Something she didn't want any of them to know about. Neither option was palatable.

Fighting his increasing feelings of unease, Travis strode swiftly to the bunkhouse. From the porch he could hear the loud raucous laughter. And the mention of Rachel's name.

"We sure fixed her, didn't we, Rowdy?"

"She'll be out there all night!"

"Stupid woman—Travis!" Rowdy pushed back his chair with a scrape. "What are you doing here?"

"Where's Rachel?" he ground out.

The hands exchanged uneasy looks. Rowdy said, "She's being initiated tonight, Travis. We, uh, well, we sent her out to look for jackalopes."

Imagining Rachel out alone, in the darkness of night, was more than Travis could take. The next thing he knew he'd crashed into the table, grabbed Rowdy by the shirtfront and was an inch from slamming a fist into his jaw. "If she's even the slightest bit hurt," he said between his teeth, "the slightest bit upset by all of this, I'm coming after you personally, you understand me?"

Rowdy's face turned beet red. He nodded.

Travis released him so hard and fast he nearly slammed into the wall. "Get this room cleaned up!" Travis ordered, his voice echoing like a thunderclap in the sudden stillness of the room. "Put the beer and the cards away."

The hands scurried to do as they were told.

Bobby Ray looked upset. "Uh, look, Travis," he said in a shaking voice, "we were just having a little bit of fun, trying to help her be one of us. We really didn't think she'd mind, 'cause she's always seemed like a good sport, at least to me, but if you want, a couple of us can go get her—"

"No." *No one was going after Rachel. No one was going to be alone with her but him.* "She's been humiliated enough. Where is she?"

"Pasture fifty-three," Bobby Ray said.

Travis turned on his heel and stormed out of the bunkhouse, the door slamming behind him. He strode to his pickup and climbed in.

His mouth set grimly, he started the engine. He didn't relish the idea of facing Rachel again after they'd recklessly made love. Never mind telling her she'd been duped.

RACHEL KNELT in the darkness, her only illumination the stars and moon. Even though the sun had gone down more than two hours ago, it was still warm and steamy, with only a hot Texas breeze to cool her. Using the back of her hand to wipe the perspiration from her brow, she finished setting the last of the thick animal nets over the burrow holes dotting the pasture, then moved back slightly, standing beside her open metal animal trap to wait.

Fifteen minutes passed. Twenty. Thirty. A half hour faded into an hour, then two, and still nothing. Only the sound of the cicadas in the trees, and the occasional hoot of an owl. Reminding herself she wasn't the only one waiting for the damned jackalopes, Rachel rubbed at the aching muscles in her shoulders and back and fought off her drowsiness.

The sound of an engine in the distance cut through the night silence and jerked Rachel back into full wakefulness. Swearing, she got to her feet. If she had to do all this again tomorrow night because some driver had made too much noise, she was really going to be ticked off.

To her surprise, it was Travis who got out of the truck. Her breath caught in her throat. Every inch of her tingled. She told herself it was because she hadn't seen him for days, and the last time she had, he'd been soaking wet, holding her against him.... No! She wouldn't think about the way they'd made love! Or the fact that he apparently had no regrets about it, while she had plenty.

His shirt gleaming in the moonlight, he came toward her. She motioned him to silence, holding an index finger to her lips. "Keep your voice down or you're going to ruin everything."

A peculiar, almost apologetic look crossed his handsome features. He drew nearer. Looking suddenly reluctant to face her, he rubbed at the back of his neck and avoided her eyes. "Rachel," he began in a near normal voice. "I've got something important to tell you."

Irritated by the way his deep sexy voice was carrying in the starlit night, Rachel stomped nearer. "Well, whatever it is can't be anywhere near as important as trapping the damned jackalopes in this pasture," she hissed. "You ought to see the damage they've done. There are holes everywhere. Watch out!" She grasped his arm above the elbow and pulled him sideways. "You almost stepped on a trap."

"So I see." He glanced down at his feet, the peculiar look still on his face. Suddenly, to her further consternation, he seemed to be fighting...laughter! "You set up fishing nets all over this field?" he asked in a strangled voice.

"They're super-strength nylon animal nets, and yes, I did," Rachel shot back impatiently. "One over every hole, along with a little bit of raw bacon for bait."

"Why?" Travis asked, his voice sounding even more strangled than it had before.

"Because if I don't catch the little critters who're doing all the burrowing, the cattle are going to fall and go lame," she explained in exasperation, surprised she would have to spell it out for him. Then again, maybe he was testing her again, to see if she really knew what she was doing.

Travis glanced back out at the empty pasture, the moonlight spilling down onto the thick dry summer grass.

She followed his glance. "Can you believe animals did all this damage?" she continued, trying hard not to notice how good he smelled, like soap and aftershave and man. Or think about how everyone else on the ranch would react if they knew she'd had sex with him. Wasn't it bad enough the two of them were fighting constantly? And yet the first time he'd actually been helpful, she'd fallen into his arms and let him make love to her as if there were no tomorrow.

"Rachel," he stated calmly. "About the other night—"

"Don't even think it. I'm not one of your little cowgirls who's just going to fall into your arms again."

"Oh, no?" He quirked a brow.

"The only thing I'm concerned about is the damned jackalopes. I'm determined to get every last one of them, even if I'm here all night!" She frowned as Travis doubled over at the waist, chuckles welling up from deep inside him.

Rachel glanced back at the nets. She was certain she'd put them out correctly, just as Rowdy and Bobby Ray had showed her. "What?" she demanded of Travis. When he didn't respond, she brushed a hand through her hair and commanded bad temperedly, "Stop laughing."

"I can't help it, Rachel…" he said, shaking his head in helpless laughter as he clutched at his abdomen and wiped the tears from his eyes.

Too late, Rachel knew what she should have sensed all along. The sick, embarrassed feeling inside her doubled. She didn't know whether to laugh or cry. She only knew she'd never felt more humiliated in her life. "I've been duped, haven't I?" she said slowly.

Travis nodded. His laughter had stopped, but the smile was still on his face, although to his credit he was trying hard to erase it completely. "I'm afraid so."

Rachel felt the blood rush from her chest, to her neck, to her face. Even her ears were hot! "About which part?" she asked dully, shame and disbelief quickly following the initial flood of embarrassment. "About how you catch a jackalope or—"

Travis put up a hand to cut her off. "There is no such thing as a jackalope."

Rachel glanced back at the rutted pasture. "Then what caused the holes?" she asked, perplexed. "Gophers?"

Again Travis shook his head. "Armadillos," he said, coming nearer. Now his laughter had stopped. "And they do need to be gotten rid of, not only because of the holes they dig and the risk that presents to any cattle, but also because they carry disease."

Rachel stared out at the pasture, not daring to look at his face for fear she'd see how stupid he really thought her. Tears stung her eyes. She told herself they were caused by sheer fatigue and not any loss of face she might feel. "You don't get rid of them using nets?" she asked.

"No," Travis said, his voice deep and soft and soothing as he moved so close to her she could feel the heat emanating from his tall body. "You put out an application of blood meal. It's an organic fertilizer available at any nursery. The stuff smells awful, but it'll work at running off the armadillos until the next rain. And the cattle won't bother it."

"Do we have any blood meal?"

Travis shrugged. "Probably not, unless Rowdy has already gone to the nursery and picked up some and spread it over the other pastures. It's not the kind of thing we keep around, because of the rancid smell, but it'll be easy enough to get. I suggest you have the men who were the most active in this prank spread it."

Rachel let out a wavering breath, glad Travis hadn't taken the opportunity to humiliate her further, but rather had seemed to try to curtail any embarrassment she felt over her own gullibility. "I'll do that," she said grimly, feeling her voice thicken as tears threatened once again. "Thanks."

Head down, she started to brush by him.

He caught her arm, his warm fingers closing over her flesh. "Rachel, I'm sorry."

So was she. More than he could ever know.

She glanced up at the moon and stars, aware the tears were running down her face now, knowing she was powerless to stop them. "The hands expected me to sit out here all night, didn't they?"

Travis didn't sugarcoat the situation. Nor did he refrain from grinning, just a bit. His hand gentling on her arm, he said softly, "They probably would have come and got you at some point."

Imagining what a joke she was to the hands, Rachel's anger flared anew and she swore, soft and low. "But in the meantime, I'm the laughingstock of the ranch," she said, then followed that with a swear word worthy of the men.

Travis let her go and leaned back against the side of the pickup. "Not the whole ranch," he reassured her, tucking his hands in the back pockets of his slacks. "My mother and the twins have no idea what they did."

"Great. That makes me feel ever so much better." Rachel shoved past him and reached blindly for the door of her pickup. She had yanked it all the way open when the next thought hit. She whirled to face him. "Were you in on this, too?"

"No." Reaching out, he grabbed her wrist, reeled her in to his side and shut the truck door. "I came out to get you as soon as I found out about it."

Rachel yanked free of him. "Thank God for small miracles," she said sarcastically.

Travis straightened until he towered over her. "Why are you mad at *me?*"

"Why not?" she ground out, turning away.

"Wait a minute." His hand shot out to grab her shoulder. "Where are you going?"

Hair flying, she spun around to face him. "Where do you think?" she railed. "The bunkhouse."

"Don't."

"Why the hell not?"

"Because we've already had one scene tonight in the bunkhouse," Travis said roughly, pulling her near again. "We don't need another."

"We've already had one scene in the bunkhouse?" she repeated, aware that when she touched him like this, body to body, her whole being still filled with tingling electrical charges. "What happened?" And why was her breathing suddenly so shallow? Why were her hands trembling? Her lips parting? Why was she wishing he'd just do what they both wanted and kiss her?

Travis's grip on her released. Reluctantly he set her slightly apart from him. His tone was gruff and somewhat apologetic. "I read Rowdy the riot act when I found out what he and the other guys had done."

She glared at him, her indignation flaming as she pictured them all standing around the bunkhouse, laughing at her. The idea of Travis storming in there like some hero rescuing a damsel in distress made it all the worse. "How dare you!"

He stared at her in consternation. "How dare I what?"

She'd been pushed over the edge once too often by all the stupid men on this stupid ranch! "It isn't enough you refuse to help me when I come to you for advice," she said. "But now, you insist on helping me when I don't want your help! And you've already seduced me into making love with you like some crazy hormone-driven teenager! Now you've undermined my authority with the men!"

He caught her arms above the elbow and held them tight. "Calm down!" he ordered, shaking her slightly.

"Don't you tell me to calm down!" Rachel shouted.

"Rachel..." he said gently.

Rachel felt a touch of panic as he continued to look at her in that kind and tender way. When he was so strong and welcoming, she was tempted to be weak and yielding.

Abruptly coming to her senses, she jerked from the warm tempting circle of his arms. It didn't matter that he kissed like no one else. She couldn't be sidetracked into making love with him again. She had her future to think about, and if she didn't find a way to make the hired hands respect her, she would never earn the right to run this ranch permanently. She would never acquire her dream!

"Just leave me alone!" she said. She'd been humiliated enough. Having him witness her downfall only made her feel worse. She regarded him coldly. "I don't need your help, and I certainly don't need your pity."

Chapter Nine

"We missed you at dinner," Travis said.

Rachel glanced up from the stack of papers in her hand. Travis was framed in the doorway of the tiny office at the front of the barn. His eyes were friendly and alert, and he looked more handsome and ruggedly appealing than ever. "I explained to your mother, and Brett and Gretchen why I couldn't be there."

"Yeah, I heard. You had to work." He sauntered into the room. "What's so critical you couldn't spare an hour to have a meal with the family?"

"We're branding the new herd tomorrow."

"So?" Travis shrugged his broad shoulders. "That's nothing the men don't already know how to do. There's no reason for you to be involved."

"I beg to differ," she said lightly, as her stomach fluttered and dropped another notch. "I think it's very important I be there."

"To assert your authority over the men?"

"Yes. Although I might add if someone on this ranch who shall go nameless set a better example, it might not be necessary."

He grinned, appearing to enjoy the obvious warmth creeping into her face. He paused and looked over her shoulder at the papers on the scarred wooden equipment table. "What are you up to?"

Rachel stared at his genuinely curious expression. She sighed heavily, letting him know she was not enjoying the unsolicited attention. "If you must know, I'm reading up on cryo-branding."

He rested one lean hip on the edge of the table. "How come?"

Unable and unwilling to be that physically close to him, she stalked over to a table of ranch gear in the corner. "Because I plan to switch to it in the near future."

Travis stalked her lazily. He braced a shoulder against the wall and slipped his hands into the back pockets of his jeans. "Isn't freeze-branding more expensive?"

"So what if it is?"

"Then why do it?" he continued as if she had answered him as politely as he had asked the question. "Unless you're trying to make this ranch go broke in record time, that is."

"It's more humane." She glared at him. "Don't you have something else to do?"

He grinned again, exerting all his charm this time. "Nope. I'm all yours for the evening, as they say."

"Great," Rachel muttered.

He watched as she tugged off her cowboy boots and pulled on high-topped barn boots. She reached for her leather gloves.

"So what are you going to use for the freeze-branding?" he asked, straightening indolently. "Liquid nitrogen, or dry ice and alcohol?"

"Liquid nitrogen," Rachel said, then paused. "Have you ever done it?"

"Nope." Travis shrugged. "I've read about it, though. Have you?"

"No, but I've seen a demonstration. I was going to go get Rowdy and ask him to assist me—you need two people to do this—but since you're already here," she decided reluctantly, "you may as well help me out."

He touched the brim of his hat, amused by her long-suffering attitude. "I'd be glad to be of service, Miss Rachel," he drawled.

Her color heightened even more. She tossed him a pair of leather gloves and protective eye wear. "Put these on," she ordered in a clipped voice. "And get a pair of barn boots. I'll meet you down at the other end of the barn."

Booted feet planted a foot apart, arms folded tightly at her waist, she was waiting for him when he appeared. "Took you long enough," she said.

"Getting dressed always does. Now, getting undressed, that's another matter entirely. I can do that pretty quick," he confided, drawing inexorably nearer, as if they were about to have a very interesting tête-à-tête. "Must have to do with—"

"Spare me the details of your love life," she interrupted.

He placed a hand flat on his chest. "Why, Rachel, I'm shocked! Who said anything about making love?"

Refusing to let him fluster her, Rachel retorted heatedly, "You're the one who mentioned getting undress— Never mind." Deciding there was no way she could benefit from furthering this conversation, she changed subjects swiftly. "Let's get down to work. Okay?"

Travis grinned as if he knew he had gotten to her. He held his gloved hands wide. "You're the boss."

She sent him a plaintive look, then handed him the leather restraint. "Would you do the honors?"

He slipped into the stall with a calf. Kneeling, he quickly restrained the frightened animal. "I thought this was so *you* could learn the ropes," he said, slipping on his protective eye wear.

"I *am* learning how to brand," Rachel retorted irritably. Still she had no desire to get into the stall and wrestle with a calf.

"I see," he said.

Ignoring his demonstrated disbelief, Rachel slipped on her own eye wear, uncapped an insulated container of liquid nitrogen, poured a small amount into a small plastic-foam cooler, then recapped the first container. "Please. No fooling around once we get started," she said.

"I'm with you there," Travis said quietly, all seriousness now as he used his gloved hand to stroke the calf into trembling submission. "That stuff is dangerous."

Rachel carried the cooler just inside the stall. "This won't hurt a bit," she soothed as she turned on the electric clippers and sheared a three-inch square on the calf's left hip. Using room-temperature alcohol and a grooming brush, she swiftly and thoroughly cleaned the area they intended to brand.

"Now what?" Travis asked, holding the calf perfectly still.

"We wet the area once more with alcohol—it's important the skin be wet when the brand is applied—and then dip the iron into the nitrogen." She moved forward to do so. "Then we apply the brand to the skin." She pressed it firmly, making sure all portions of the Bar W brand were in contact with the hide, then held it for fifty seconds. "Done," Rachel said, removing the brand.

"The skin looks frozen," Travis remarked, studying the brand.

"In a couple hours it'll become swollen and look like frostbite," Rachel said. Rising carefully, she exited the stall, carrying the brand and cooler of liquid nitrogen.

"Then what?" Travis asked, unbuckling the trembling calf from the leather restraint. With the back of his hand, he stroked the side of the calf's face gently, lovingly.

Rachel forced her eyes away from the tender ministrations of his hands and back to his face, trying not to think about how good it had felt to have those same hands sensuously stroking her body. "In about twenty days, the hair around the brand will have completely fallen out. When it comes back in again, it'll come in white, because the nitrogen will have destroyed the pigment cells in the skin," she explained. She held what remained of the liquid nitrogen in the cooler carefully away from her chest.

"And that's it, huh?" Travis shoved back his protective eye wear, so it rested on top of his head.

"Yeah." Rachel nodded. She stepped back in the aisleway, allowing him room to open the door of the stall and slip out, too. "The cow will be branded for life."

Suddenly, as Rachel watched in stunned surprise, the calf bolted. It tried to dart between Travis's legs. Travis simultaneously tripped over the calf and pushed the animal. In a split second, Travis lunged forward, then attempted to regain his balance. His shoulder banged the stall door. And the stall door hit Rachel. The next thing she knew the liquid nitrogen had splashed up and hit the front of her blouse.

Knowing there was no time to spare, Rachel quickly put down the container and with one fierce yanking motion ripped her blouse open. Buttons flew. Travis slammed the stall door shut behind him and leapt forward to help her struggle out of the splattered cloth.

"Are you hurt?" he demanded as her ripped shirt fluttered to the barn floor.

"No. I...I don't think so," Rachel said shakily, glancing down. None of the ninety-degree-below-zero liquid had touched her skin.

She shoved her own eye wear up to get a better look at her chest. Her transparent bra would hardly have afforded her much protection.

Beside her, Travis let out a ragged breath. "Thank God," he said.

Suddenly Rachel became aware, as did he, that she was standing there half-naked.

Thinking quickly, he shrugged out of his shirt. Next thing she knew the denim fabric was wrapped around her, enclosing her in the warm male scent of him. As heady as the scent assaulting her nostrils was the gallant way he held the edges of the cloth together, closing off her trembling body from view. "That was close," he said. "Too close."

Rachel's head tipped back. She'd come very near to being scarred for life. She trembled. "I agree."

He looked down at her. "Rachel..." he said, his voice low, hoarse, raw.

The next thing she knew his arms were around her, holding her tightly against him, and they were kissing. Only this time wasn't like the first time or the second. This time there was even less restraint...and more hot searing passion. He was so utterly male, so strong, so insistent. He made her want to open up, to absorb him and take in every nuance.

Her hands moved to his neck, then lower, to the smooth skin and endless muscles of his bare back. She hadn't known she could be so greedy, but she was. She hadn't known anything could feel this good, but it did. She moved against him, up and into him, not caring that with her movements his shirt fell down around her shoulders, not caring that all that stood between them from the waist up was one thin transparent scrap of cloth.

His hand swept to her breast, cupped it. The crown raised against his hot seeking flesh. His hand moved to her other breast, sweetly exploring. And still they kissed, until she no longer knew where her mouth ended and his began. Only that she had waited all of her adult life for someone, something like this, to happen to her.

He groaned as she let her fingertips work down his spine and pressed her into him all the more urgently, until her breasts were flattened against the hard planes of his chest and she ached to know more fully the hot ridge of his desire. The yearning pressure of his mouth increased, so alluring and wonderfully evocative, until all the strength sapped out of her legs and she trembled with the promise of more.

He paused long enough to glance over his shoulder at the emptiness of the barn. One arm slid beneath her knees. He swept her up into his arms, crumpled shirt and all, and carried her the short distance to the tack room. And it was then, as he set her down in front of the scarred table, that she fully realized what was happening.

The heat of her embarrassment flooded her face. She couldn't believe they'd been about to do this again. They were in a barn, for pity's sake. She was the manager of this ranch! She couldn't—especially not in the barn. Sweet heaven, what had she been thinking?

"No, Travis, stop," she gasped, flattening a palm against his chest.

"What do you mean, no?" he rasped, his hands resting on her bare shoulders. "That didn't feel like any no I've ever experienced!"

She pushed away from him and struggled into his shirt. "We can't do this, Travis." She tried to fasten the buttons despite her trembling.

"Why not?"

"Because it's a mistake, that's why," Rachel said. "Just like the last time was a mistake." She tried to make a cool controlled move toward the door.

He was quicker, cooler still, moving just as resolutely to block her way. "I don't play games, Rachel."

"Neither do I."

"Oh?"

"I'm not playing games," she protested. "I just came to my senses." *Thank heaven!*

"But not before you kissed me like that. Like—!"

She shoved the hair from her eyes with both hands. "I made a mistake, okay?"

"No, it's not okay," he said softly. His slate-blue eyes were fierce. "Whether you want to admit it or not, what we did just now was right." His glance skimmed her mouth lovingly before returning to her eyes. "Nothing in this world ever felt so right to me."

Nor to me, Rachel thought. But she also knew that wasn't the point. "So we acted impulsively!" How could she have let herself be so vulnerable with him? "But how will you feel about this tomorrow, Travis, in the cold light of day?" Tears sparkled in her eyes. "What will people say when they find out you've taken up with your late brother's wife?"

His jaw clenched. "They won't find out."

Recognition dawned, making her feel even more bitter and self-righteous. "Oh, I get it now. You want me to be your secret and oh-so-convenient, live-in, closemouthed mistress."

"You don't have to be so crude!" he said without an ounce of his previous tenderness.

"Why not?" Rachel shot back. "It's the truth. You want me to be with you and keep my mouth shut."

His eyes pierced hers. Rachel gulped, knowing she'd gone too far. Too late, he was already focusing on her mouth and yanking her against him. Though Rachel struggled against it, she could feel the fierceness of his desire against her middle.

"Not necessarily," he replied in a soft sarcastic voice. "I can think of plenty of things—" he touched his lips to hers lightly "—to do with that beautiful mouth of yours, besides shut it."

"*You're* crude!"

"And you're a liar if you're trying to tell me you don't enjoy my lovemaking," he whispered. "Or that you don't want me again tonight!"

Fighting the charges of electricity that arrowed through her, Rachel twisted out of his grasp. "I won't be your secret mistress."

Travis leaned against the door frame and folded his arms across his chest. "To call you my mistress would be to believe you're less than my equal, Rachel," he said gently. "And you're not."

Their eyes met. Rachel's throat ached.

"And I want you to be my lover, my equal-in-every-way lover," he said. He moved to take her tenderly in his arms once again. "I want that very much."

Rachel rested her head against his chest, hating to admit how close she was to giving in. There were times when she detested him, but there were also times, like now, when she knew she'd never felt more drawn to any man. "Mistress. Lover," she said bitterly, as his hand gently stroked her back. "It all boils down to the same thing." *I may be falling in love with you. And you, Travis, want me.*

"Not in my mind, it doesn't," Travis whispered. "A mistress is a kept woman. A lover is someone who pulls her own weight, and that, Rachel," he said softly, "you do very nicely."

Although that was the closest Travis had ever come to giving her a compliment about the way she ran the ranch, she refused to let his soft seductive soothing words sway her. Pushing away from him, she gathered up her ruined shirt.

He caught her around the waist. They were aligned firmly hip to hip, torso to torso. His body was hard and unyielding, but his voice was soft and soothing. "I understand you're scared," he said sympathetically. "I didn't expect the passion, either. But we can work it out."

"Come to an agreement," she paraphrased dryly, sensing another deal in the making. What would he offer her to be his lover? she wondered. A permanent home on the ranch as long as they were together? Or just a room in town?

"Exactly," Travis agreed practically. "We can find some way to be with each other that's comfortable for both of us."

The only thing that would make Rachel comfortable was marriage. And that, he wasn't offering. She stared at him, wishing they'd met some other time, some other way, and that she had never had her reputation compromised by her hasty ill-thought-out marriage to his brother. "Assuming we could deal with a scandal should one—"

"We could."

"And my kids and your mother?"

"We could manage them, too."

"And find a way to be together—"

"Yes."

"Just how 'comfortable' will any of this be if I earn the right to run this ranch from now on?"

His face whitened. He said nothing. But then he didn't have to. She could see how he felt. "You'd never forgive me, would you?"

Still, he said nothing.

"Don't you see, Travis?" Inside, she felt as if her heart was breaking. "The ranch will always be between us, and even if it wasn't, there's always the ghost of Austin."

He was quiet. "Why are you so quick to write us off?"

"Because there is no 'us,' Travis," she said. "Only a temporary lapse in judgment."

Travis's mouth thinned. "As you see it..."

"I'm determined not to repeat it."

His jaw clenched with the effort it took to rein in his temper. "Right. I forgot," he said with deliberate cruelty. "A romance with me might get in the way of your ultimate goals."

"Travis..." she began, feeling weary to her soul. But it was too late—he was already stalking out of the barn. And this time, he didn't look back.

RACHEL SNEAKED into the kitchen the back way. Jaclyn gasped, her gaze moving from Rachel's oversized shirt to the ruined one in her hand. "Goodness, darling, what happened?"

Rachel stopped dead in her tracks, an embarrassed flush heating her cheeks. "I spilled some liquid nitrogen on my shirt. So Travis lent me his."

Jaclyn paled. "Were you hurt?"

"No, thank goodness," Rachel replied with genuine relief. "But I know I should have been more careful. I will be in the future." And would have been tonight had she not been concentrating so much on Travis and his sexy handsome presence, instead of what she was doing, Rachel scolded herself silently.

"Was Travis helping you?"

"Yes." Rachel prayed she didn't look as if she had just been thoroughly kissed. So thoroughly she was still feeling the tingles. She forced herself to turn around and meet Jaclyn's concerned gaze. "He wanted to see how cryo-branding was done."

"Oh. That sounds interesting," Jaclyn said. "Do you think it will work out?"

"Oh, yes." Rachel smiled, then realized Jaclyn was watching her. "Something on your mind?"

"I just wondered if you and Travis had another quarrel."

"Not exactly," Rachel hedged. "Why?"

"He seemed rather upset."

So am I, Rachel thought. She and Travis couldn't continue like this. Yet it was impossible to be so close to him and not desire him. "Where is he?" she asked casually, turning her thoughts away from the passionate kisses they had shared. Had they been anywhere else but the barn...no, she wouldn't think about what might have happened.

"That's just it. I don't know." Jaclyn frowned. "He stormed in like a heathen, went upstairs, grabbed a clean shirt, came back down and announced he was going out for the evening.''

Rachel swore silently. It was clear she was going to have to find some way to talk to him and smooth things over. "Oh. Well, he deserves an evening out."

"And you deserve a hot meal, as hard as you've been working," Jaclyn said with maternal concern. "Sit down and let me fix you a plate."

Rachel forced another smile as her inner turmoil grew. "I really should change..." She gestured at Travis's denim shirt, still warm and scented with the fragrance of his cologne and the heady masculine smell of his skin.

"Nonsense. You look fine. Beside, there's something I wanted to ask you about Brett and Gretchen." Jaclyn put a plate of steaming food in front of Rachel. "You know Maria is taking a week off to visit her daughter in California, starting Monday."

Rachel glanced up from her chicken-fried steak and mashed potatoes. "She mentioned it to me this morning, yes."

"I usually take time away from the ranch during Maria's vacation, too. But this year, instead of going to Galveston to visit friends, I'd like to take the twins to Florida to visit Disney World, Busch Gardens, maybe even the Keys. What do you think?"

"I think that would be wonderful," she said slowly, meaning it. If only she could have a change of pace, too. But as Travis had reminded her so many times, she had a ranch to run.

Chapter Ten

"Bye!"

"Have a wonderful time!" Rachel and Travis shouted as they waved. They stood shoulder to shoulder in front of the Bar W airstrip, watching the chartered Texas West Airlines jet taxi and take off.

As soon as the jet disappeared from view, Travis spun on his heel and swaggered back to the Cadillac they'd driven out to the airstrip. He jerked open the door in a way that let Rachel know he hadn't completely forgiven her for calling a halt that night in the barn. Not yet. Nor was she sure she wanted him to. Maybe it was safer for both of them if he stayed angry with her.

Travis started the Cadillac with a vengeance and backed out of the shade next to the hangar. "You don't have to look so thrilled," he finally grumbled. "Besides—" he jabbed a thumb at the center of his chest, while continuing to steer the smooth-riding luxury car with the other hand "—I'm the one who should be upset."

Rachel turned to face him, thinking that, as angry as she was with him, she still liked the way he looked in jeans. Like a real cowboy. "You?" she demanded. "Why?"

His lower jaw jutted forward. He slanted her an aggrieved glance, then finished in a low grim thoroughly exasperated tone, "Because I know what my mother is up to, even if you don't."

Rachel shot him a confused look.

"My mother saw me come in without my shirt a couple of nights ago."

"So? She saw me come in wearing it!" And probably, Rachel thought morosely, knowing Jaclyn's keen eye and superb people-sense, she had also realized that Travis had steadfastly avoided being alone with Rachel ever since.

"Which probably also means she figured out for herself what happened," Travis said.

Rachel didn't like being reminded of the way she'd responded to his kiss or how close they had come to making love again. If they'd been anywhere but the barn, if the ranch hadn't been standing between them . . . But it was, she reminded herself firmly, then and now! And so was Travis's continued resentment of her. "How do you know that?"

"I just do."

Hating his confidence in the face of such an indelicate situation, Rachel stared at him through narrowed eyes. "You didn't tell her that you kissed me, did you?"

Travis guided the car around the circular drive and halted it in front of the house. He cut the engine and turned to her. "What we shared was a heck of a lot more than a simple kiss." Merriment tugged at the corners of his mouth and his teeth flashed white. "At least the way I recall it."

Unfortunately, that was the way Rachel recalled it, too. She quelled the urge to fidget in the plush leather seat and decided to have this out with him, in the car, in broad daylight, in front of the ranch house rather than inside it. "Go on," she instructed flatly.

"So I'm not playing her game." Travis shrugged.

"Which is?"

He gave her a droll look. "You really haven't figured this out?"

"What?" Rachel's pulse quickened.

Travis studied her intimately. "Okay. She knows you're unhappy here."

"I am *not* unhappy!" Rachel protested. "I love running the ranch."

"Unhappy with me," he specified, his exasperated voice overriding hers. "And that you're lonely and isolated."

Rachel couldn't deny she missed the company of other adults. Since the jackalope fiasco, the ranch hands had been increasingly nicer to her and more respectful, maybe because she hadn't punished anyone, but they still weren't exactly her friends. Yet. "And?"

Travis rubbed at his thigh with the flat of his palm. "And she wants me to make you feel better."

Rachel tossed her head. "The only way you could possibly do that is if you went back to Fort Worth."

Travis slammed out of the car, circled around the front and opened the passenger door. "First of all, there's no way that'll happen as long as you're here," he drawled.

Rachel propelled herself into the hot sun. "How nice to know you trust me," she shot back sweetly, heading for the shade of the front porch.

"Second, she has no intention of my leaving." Travis ate up the distance between them. "In fact," he continued, thrusting his key into the lock on the front door, "my leaving you is the farthest thing from her mind."

Rachel rolled her eyes, exasperated. "I still haven't the foggiest idea what you're talking about." He swung open the door and she went inside.

"She's matchmaking!"

Rachel whirled to face him. She planted her hands on her hips. "Now I know you're crazy!"

Travis studied her grimly. "We both only wish. The truth is she loves you like a daughter and she's crazy about the kids."

Heat and panic combined sent strange vibrations through her entire body. She inhaled a short gasping breath. "I was married to your brother!"

"And my brother is dead," Travis replied gruffly. "In a few years, the twins'll be off to college. You'll be alone. And she figures you'll probably marry again. If it's to someone outside the family, Mom knows chances are she'll lose you again. She doesn't want that to happen."

"I still don't see where you come into all this," Rachel said, telling herself sternly that what he was intimating couldn't be true.

"Don't you?" Travis gave her a steady look that robbed every drop of moisture from her mouth.

Deciding too much had been said, she tried to exit the front hall. He put his hand over hers, preventing her escape.

Knowing from experience that this conversation was not going to be over until he'd said all he had to say, Rachel stilled.

"She wants me to step in and personally fill that husbandly void in your life. Fortunately for both of us—" Travis released his hold on her abruptly "—I'm just not interested in marriage. Period. Nor do I have any intention of putting myself in Austin's shadow. I spent far too much time doing that as a kid."

He strode in the direction of his office. Rachel stared after him, then decided as far as she was concerned, their conversation wasn't finished. When she caught up with him, he was seated in front of his computer.

"I don't understand. Did you do that out of hero worship? Out of choice?" Rachel tried to soften her voice, wanting to understand just what it was that had driven Travis to live in Austin's shadow.

Travis typed in a command on the keyboard and didn't look at her. "More like obligation. And parental expectation." He hit the Enter key with more than necessary force, then swiveled to face her. "For as long as I can recall, I was expected to do the same extracurricular activities, take the same kind of lessons, enroll in the same business, economic and agricultural classes at the same university. After Austin's death, I even picked up the slack by helping run the ranch." He pushed away from the chair and began to pace the tiny room. "But I am not," he warned as he clamped both powerful forearms over his chest, "repeat, *am not,* going to do this, too."

"How reassuring," she said dryly, determined to cover her hurt, "to know my virtue is safe with you."

"Now that, I didn't say."

For a moment her lungs stopped functioning.

"Your heart is safe with me, as is your single-woman status," he corrected. "About the rest—" he grinned at her with bad-boy panache "—we'll have to see."

"Get this through your head, Travis. I'm not going to become your lover."

"Time will tell, won't it?" he assured her confidently. "Should I expect you for dinner?"

Rachel glowered and gave him a brief parody of a smile. "Not on your life, cowboy."

BECAUSE SHE KNEW he normally liked to eat at seven, Rachel barricaded herself in her office, then went out to supervise the work of the hands. She waited until nine to journey to the kitchen.

To her dismay, Travis was still there, slouched low in his chair, his booted feet propped up on the seat of another chair, a long-necked bottle of beer in his hand. The aroma of simmering spices and beef filled the air.

He tipped his hat at her, drawling, "Don't you look surprised."

"I thought you'd be done by now," Rachel responded tartly.

"Would've been, if I hadn't had to cook," Travis said, taking another sip of beer. He looked at her and grinned, enjoying every ounce of her discomfiture. She ignored the pot simmering on the stove and looked inside the refrigerator.

"Actually," Travis continued lazily, watching as she took a frozen microwave dinner from the freezer compartment, "I was hoping you'd cook for me."

Rachel set the frozen dinner down with a thud. "Dream on."

He watched her pull the makings of a salad from the well-stocked fridge. "I tell you what. I'll make you a deal."

"Oh, yeah?" Rachel had to climb over his legs to get to the sink.

"I'll share my chili, if you share your salad."

Rachel wasn't of a mind to cooperate with him. Unfortunately she was starving, and his chili was much more tempting than the frozen entrée she'd just gotten out of the freezer. "Is it edible?"

"Cross my heart." He gave her his best choirboy look. "Come on, Rachel. I'm trying to declare a cease-fire. After all, we're going to be alone here all week."

He had a point, Rachel admitted grudgingly. She hated arguing. This was a chance for them to become friends and for her to persuade him she not only could but should run the ranch. "I suppose it would be okay," she relented. "This once."

Having gotten his way, he sent her a tantalizing grin and his feet hit the floor with an energetic thud. He went to the pantry and began rummaging around, finally emerging with a yellow package of cornmeal, which he tossed from palm to palm. "You know how to make corn bread?"

"Yes." She drew out the word carefully, not about to start waiting on him hand and foot, truce or no.

His dark brows lifted hopefully. "The old-fashioned, cooked-in-a-cast-iron-skillet kind? You know, that you make on top of the stove?"

"Yes."

He took off his hat and set it aside, then approached her in all seriousness. "Will you show me how? After you finish the salad, of course."

The thought of corn bread spread with butter was too good to pass up. Rachel left the greens on the sideboard. "The corn bread will take a while," she warned. "We better start it first."

Together they got out the ingredients.

"You sure are good at this," Travis remarked, as he watched her mix the ingredients. "How come you never married again?"

Rachel put some butter into the microwave to melt. "Who says I didn't?" she asked contrarily.

"Did you?" When the microwave dinged, Travis reached in to get the dish.

"No." Rachel added the melted butter to the dry ingredients in the bowl.

"Why not?"

"Because of the twins. I would never marry someone unless he loved them as much as I do."

"Surely there are men out there who'd love the twins?"

Yes, but they don't love me. Not the way I want and need to be loved. "What about you?" Rachel asked as she broke an egg. "You've never married."

"Says who?"

She turned with a start, irritated to find how jealous she felt at just the thought of Travis's marrying someone else. "Have you?"

He grinned at her and reached over to add the buttermilk to the bowl. "No."

"Why not?" She told herself the acceleration of her heartbeat and the dampness of her palms was just due to the challenge of matching wits with him.

Travis took the bowl from her and began to stir the batter. "It's not easy finding a woman to love you for you alone, when she sees all this. And then," he sighed, "there's my airlines, too."

Rachel buttered the bottom of a cast-iron skillet. "You're more than the sum total of your financial assets."

"That's what I keep telling the ladies." Travis smiled. "How did we get onto this subject, anyway?"

"You were nosing around in my private life, as usual." Rachel poured the batter into the skillet and then placed it on the burner.

"And you weren't nosing around in mine?"

She handed him a carrot to peel. "Can we drop this?"

"Sure. What do you want to talk about?"

What's safe? She couldn't think about his looks or the way he kissed or the desire that kept surging within her every time she was close to him. If she didn't know better, she'd think . . . No. She was not foolish enough to actually let herself fall in love with a confirmed bachelor. It was just desire she was feeling. The forbidden element of their infatuation.

"Oh, well, at least my mother got what she wanted."

Afraid he could read the direction of her not-so-innocent thoughts, Rachel flushed guiltily.

"The two of us alone," Travis continued affably. "She probably figures in a week we'll either kill each other, start a romance or declare a permanent truce."

She wouldn't even consider a romance with him. As for the truce, he didn't know how good it sounded to her. And yet, a truce would deprive her of the prickliness that had served as her emotional armor. A truce might open the way to... their previous recklessness.

"Or don't you want a permanent cease-fire?"

She shrugged and kept her face inscrutable. "Maybe."

He gave her one of his Texas bad-boy grins. "Like to tangle with me, don't you?" he prodded in a low sexy tone.

Rachel ignored the chill that chased down her spine. "It breaks up the monotony."

He touched a hand to the side of her face. "The monotony or the loneliness?" he asked softly.

He was too close for comfort. "Maybe a little of both," Rachel allowed.

His hand slid around to the nape of her neck. He drew nearer still.

Her heart pounding, Rachel stepped back.

"Aw, come on, Rachel. Don't run from me." His other hand came up to rub her back tenderly. "Don't run from this."

"Travis, I..." She tried to move away from the hand on her spine, but she succeeded only in bringing her breasts into contact with the hard muscles of his chest. It was all she could do to suppress the moan welling up in her throat.

His eyes darkened. Fire raged through her. He brought her up on tiptoe, and then his mouth touched hers. He gave her a kiss that was so gentle, so reverent, so coaxing, it left her weak. Her breath whispered out unevenly. They kissed again, this time with

much more courage, her lips yielding to the hard demanding pressure of his.

He released her but didn't step back. "I won't push
you. I won't lie to you, either." His eyes probed hers,
searching for understanding. "I want to make love to
you," he whispered. "I want it so bad I lie awake
nights imagining how your body would tremble beneath my hands. And I want you to make love to me."
He tangled his fingers in her hair and leaned forward
to give her one last, soft, kiss. She was trembling when
he drew back. And she trembled even more as he said,
"And that, Rachel, is not going to change. No matter
how much you ignore it, no matter how much you ignore me, the passion between us is not going to go
away."

RACHEL PUNCHED her pillow for the hundredth time
and tried to get comfortable in the four-poster bed, but
it was no use. She couldn't stop thinking of Travis, in
his own bed, just down the hall.

Damn him, anyway. Every time she started to think
they might be friends, Travis went and pulled something like that. Why did he have to be so relentless
about going after what he wanted?

His relentless desire intrigued her and scared her.
She wanted him to court her. She wanted to please
him. She wanted them to be friends. Maybe more than
friends. And at the same time, she knew he was only
interested in an affair at best.

Besides, he was her ex-brother-in-law, for pity's sake. The only problem was she couldn't think of him that way any longer. She knew, as sad as it was, after the way he'd kissed her tonight, so sweetly, lingeringly and persuasively, that she never would again.

"THIS IS UNDOUBTEDLY going to be the longest week of my life," Rachel muttered the next morning as she began to fix herself some toast for breakfast. It didn't help, of course, that it had seemed to take forever for her to fall asleep and when she finally did she'd dreamed of Travis, of the heat of his kisses and the fervency of his desire. She awoke near dawn, drenched in sweat and aching in places she would much have preferred not to ache.

"Do you always talk to yourself when you're alone? And why is it going to be the longest week of your life?" Travis asked as he strolled into the kitchen.

"No, I don't always talk to myself although maybe I should," Rachel said gruffly, catching a whiff of his freshly showered body as he brushed past her to get to the coffee.

He looked askance at her empty plate. "No eggs?" He looked disappointed.

"There are plenty," she bit out. "In the refrigerator."

"That's a thought. A Rocky-style breakfast, downed raw. Shall I get you a couple and break them into a glass?"

Rachel thought she would be ill if she had to look at a couple of raw eggs sitting in a glass, never mind watching anyone actually drink them. Worse, she felt Travis might just do that if he thought it would get a rise out of her. She gave him her back. "Suit yourself."

"You sure are prickly in the morning," he observed.

She glowered at him over her shoulder, irritated she couldn't get a moment's peace. "Maybe it's the company."

He grinned unrepentantly. "Maybe." Still grinning, he removed a carton of orange juice from the refrigerator. "You know, you don't look as if you slept too well."

"Yeah, well, you look like you slept incredibly well," she grumbled.

"Yep, as a matter of fact, I did. Want to know what I dreamed about?"

"No!"

His eyes gleamed with mischief. "I could tell you—"

"I'm sure you have better things to do," she interrupted.

"Not really. The summer airfare wars are winding down, and we already have our travel rates set for fall. Plus, travel is up in general in late August and September, mostly because of all the kids going back to college, so..."

"I'm glad you're doing so well," she said.

He leaned against the counter and sipped his juice. "What about you? How are things going?"

That, Rachel would rather not talk about. "Things are about as I expected them to be."

"Given up on raising organic beef yet?"

"No."

"Find a buyer for the herd you already have?"

I'm working on it, Rachel thought. "I will," she assured him.

He grinned.

If she didn't know better, Rachel thought, she'd think Travis was actually beginning to root for her, despite his own interests in the matter. But that couldn't be happening, could it? Not when he was so determined to hold on to the ranch.

Her toast popped up. Eager to be out of his way, she grabbed the two pieces and flipped them onto her plate, burning her fingers slightly in the process.

Before she could react, he grabbed her fingers and blew on them. "You know, some say butter is the best thing for a burn, smoothed on nice and slick, but it's actually the worst thing to use. What you need is ice-cold water." He dragged her hand over to the tap and pushed it beneath the running faucet. "See how that cools the skin?"

And how his touch heated it just as quickly, she thought.

She jerked her hand away from his and attempted to look as calm and collected and faintly mocking as he did. "Thanks for the first-aid lesson," she said dryly.

"We aim to please." His eyes held hers for a long moment before he looked at her plate and frowned. "Is that really all you're having?"

"And coffee."

"I thought you'd know how to cook, having kids and all."

Rachel carried her plate to the table and sat down. "I do know how to cook," she reminded him in exasperation. Realizing she'd forgotten the jam, she got up and headed for the cupboards over the counter, making sure to give him wide berth. "I made the salad and taught you how to make corn bread last night, remember?"

"Oh, yeah," Travis drawled, as he watched her search the shelves. "Guess that slipped my mind in light of all the *other* important things that went on."

Refusing to dignify his innuendo with either a reply or a blush, Rachel carried the jam, when she found it, back to the table. Unfortunately the jar was brand-new and wouldn't open, no matter how she tried.

"You're not doing so well opening that jam, either."

"That's because it won't open," Rachel said between gritted teeth.

He swaggered closer. "You forgot to take off the plastic safety seal around the lid. Gotta do that first, Rachel. Then you can open it."

"I know that," she said irritably, picking at the seal with her third finger.

"Getting a headache?"

"No!"

Suddenly, he was massaging her shoulders and neck. "Sure you're feeling all right?"

"Yes. Wonderful. Or at least I was before you showed up and *invaded my space.*"

He laughed. Using the pressure he exerted on her shoulders, he whirled her around to face him. "Lady, I haven't even begun to invade your space." He leaned down until their eyes were level. "And trust me, you'll *know* when I have."

She knew he wanted her to fight with him. He wanted her to haul off and hit him. He wanted her emotions to be out of control, so he'd have an excuse to drag her into his arms and kiss her thoroughly. Well, she wasn't going to play his game. Fighting for calm Rachel closed her eyes and took a deep breath. "Travis, I have not yet had my coffee and—"

"Oh. One of those." He clucked sympathetically. "Just stay right where you are. I'll get you a cup. How do you like it? Cream only, right?"

Rachel buried her face in her hands. This week was going to seem like a year! "Right," she said weakly.

He set it in front of her. It was just the way she liked it, with double cream.

Travis poured himself a cup and strolled over to open the kitchen blinds. Sunlight streamed into the room. "You know, I always felt sorry for people who couldn't wake up until they'd had their coffee. Seems like a waste of a good half hour or so, you know?''

Rachel sipped her coffee and closed her eyes, still groggy from lack of sleep. ''I have a feeling you'd wake anyone up.''

''Right about that. When I set my mind to it, that is.'' His voice dropped a seductive notch. Although she hadn't yet opened her eyes, she could feel him studying her. ''Are you sure you're feeling all right?''

No, she wasn't feeling all right, she thought. He'd turned her life upside down. And she had the feeling that his campaign to get her into his bed had just begun.

''I'm fine,'' she said. ''I just . . . I miss the twins.'' And that was the truth! She hadn't been spending nearly enough time with them. But that would change, too, just as soon as she secured their inheritance for them.

''I know,'' Travis sympathized gently. ''I miss them, too. But I'm sure they're having a wonderful time.''

Rachel finished her coffee, got up and placed her cup in the sink. ''I know.'' If only her life were as serene and well-ordered as her children's seemed to be at this moment.

Travis, mistaking her glum look, joined her at the sink and started to console her by taking her in his arms. Rachel jumped back.

''Now what?''

Rachel ran her hands through her hair, wishing she'd had the foresight to tie the freshly shampooed strands back in some tight unappealing fashion, rather than leaving her hair down around her shoulders. "Look, Travis, despite the window of opportunity you undoubtedly see here, I am not going to allow myself to be seduced again," she began heatedly. "I'm not a foolish kid anymore. I don't confuse physical desire with the reality of making my everyday life work. I am not going to fall into the same trap twice."

"Meaning what?"

"Meaning I am not going to have an affair with you just to make my life easier!"

He stomped nearer, blazing with anger. "You think that's all this is? Convenience? You think that's what I want? Just the first piece of, er, available woman?"

Rachel lifted her chin and glared at him stormily. "I don't think you've gotten much past easing the ache in your groin!"

He flinched.

As his eyes darkened with hurt, she was filled with guilt. "I'm sorry," she apologized. She held up both hands in a gesture of surrender. "I'm insulting you and I don't mean to. You're a very handsome and sexy and appealing man, okay? But I am not, I repeat, *not*, in the market for an affair!"

He sent her a hot amused look. "You don't kiss like you're not in the market for an affair."

"I fail to see how—"

"You kiss like you're a woman who needs to be loved well and often, by a man who knows what he's doing."

Her heart pounding, Rachel stood her ground. "And I suppose that's you."

He inclined his head and lowered his mouth to hers, so their lips were but a millimeter away. "I think I'm in the running."

Rachel jerked her head back and stepped away. "And I think you have an ego the size of a Mack truck!"

He shrugged. "At least I'm honest."

"I'm trying to be honest with you!" she said.

He stepped back and clamped his arms across his powerful chest. "No," he corrected. "You're trying to ignore what's happening between us. And you're furious because *I* won't let you."

Rachel pretended little interest. "All right. You're right about this much. I do find you desirable, Travis. But I'm not going to act on that desire. Your family means too much to me. Jaclyn has become the loving mother I never had. I care about her."

"So what does that have to do with us and the fireworks we feel when we kiss? Why do we have to drag the kids or my mother or even the ownership of the ranch into that?"

She took a deep breath, wanting more than anything to fashion some sort of workable truce with him. "Because passion fades. We both know that."

His brow lifted in obvious disagreement. "The hell we do!"

Rachel set her chin stubbornly. "I won't risk the happiness I've found here at the ranch for a love affair with you."

His face changed. He looked away for a long moment, then back at her. Too late, she saw she'd hurt him—badly.

"Fine. Have it your way. Be alone the rest of your life for all I care."

Chapter Eleven

That afternoon, Travis sat in his Fort Worth office. His secretary had left hours ago, but he was reluctant to follow suit. The condo he'd called home for the past seven years no longer had much appeal for him. And he couldn't go back to the ranch. Rachel was there. Rachel . . .

She'd become such a large part of his life. Such an important part. He'd told himself initially that he was just protecting his own interests by keeping such close tabs on her. But somehow, as the summer had progressed, all that had changed. He'd started to enjoy her company and feel he could confide in her. Their familial connection aside, he had started to *like* her and want her as a friend. And that disturbed him greatly.

He still wasn't sure he should trust her. And yet, he knew deep down that he did. She would never deliberately hurt his family or the ranch, though she might do so without meaning to. And as for her being cut out to run the ranch, a person only had to be with her for five minutes to know that she was so enamored of the Bar W, and indeed every nitty-gritty detail of ranching, that she could run it. A strong independent businesswoman, she was feisty, hardheaded and possessed too much gumption for her own good. Of course, some of her experiments, like organically raised cattle, were bound to fail. But others like freeze-branding might succeed.

He couldn't fault her work habits. She was up early and went to bed late almost every day. She loved his mother and was an excellent mother to her own children. She seemed to revel in the extended family— having three generations under one roof. She belonged there. Sometimes, to his immense irritation, more than he did himself.

Heat radiated through him as he recalled how Rachel's lips had felt under his—sweet, giving and inventive. And he knew he'd had just a taste of her ability to surrender. But he might never be given the chance to make love to her again, or to find out more about her most private thoughts and feelings.

What would have happened had he and Rachel not been in the barn the night she'd spilled the liquid nitrogen on her shirt? What if they'd been somewhere else, somewhere private, with a bed? Would she have let him make love to her, as he'd sensed she yearned to do? Would she have said to hell with everything else and given in to her feelings, or would she have continued to hold him at arm's length? And why did the thought of either possibility leave him in such a vaguely disgruntled mood? Hadn't he already made a decision to cut her out of his life, at least the romantic part?

Even now, when he was upset with her for putting on the brakes, he still wanted her in bed with him, where she belonged, her body warm and pliant and giving beneath his, her fiery red hair spread out like silk on his pillow. He still wanted to sleep with her wrapped in his arms all night. He wanted, he admitted with gut-wrenching honesty, what he could never have, what he had no right to want—his late brother's wife.

Was he falling into the same trap he had in his youth? Was he unconsciously, dutifully, molding his life into the shape of his brother's? Travis knew it might seem that way to outsiders. But after much reflection, he knew it wasn't true. He knew it was time to put all that aside, to stop worrying about what Austin had done or not and start working on his own future.

And like it or not, he had changed since Rachel had entered his life. His business was no longer enough to keep him happy. He needed more. And he thought now he would get it.

"IT CAN'T BE that bad. *Can* it?"

The sound of the low sexy voice brought Rachel's head up. The joy she felt at seeing Travis again after his absence was muted by the despair she felt over her work. One thing was certain, though. Rachel couldn't deal with another seduction attempt. She lowered her head to the cluttered surface of her desk again and moaned, "Go away, Travis."

"Hey there," he chided good-naturedly, not bothering to disguise the sensuality that smoldered beneath his gaze. "Is that any way to greet a person you haven't seen in five days?"

"It's the only way I'm going to," Rachel said stubbornly. Her bad temper, she knew, was her only defense against him. "Now go away."

"Sorry. No can do." He crossed to her desk and scooping up a handful of papers, he cleared a space and sat on it. "You don't look too good, you know that?"

"Thanks for telling me." Inhaling his scent was like receiving an injection of adrenaline.

"Matter of fact, you haven't been getting a whole lot of sleep lately."

And he looked disgustingly rested, Rachel thought.

The truth was, she *hadn't* been getting a whole lot of sleep. For a variety of reasons. She kept thinking about Travis and what they could have if only so many things didn't stand between them. Not wanting him to know how vulnerable she was where he was concerned, she propped her feet casually on the edge of her desk. "What brings you back to the Bar W? I thought you were going to stay in Fort Worth until Jaclyn and the twins returned."

"They're coming back early this afternoon instead of late tonight. Apparently the twins miss you desperately. They said they tried to call you, but the phone was busy."

"I have been on the phone since early this morning," she said.

He scrutinized her carefully. "Are you sure you're okay? You look like you've been through the wringer."

Rachel kneaded the knotted muscles in the back of her neck with both hands. "Maybe because sending five hundred head of cattle to market is no easy task."

"Yeah. I heard you've been doing that this week," he said sympathetically. "I saw Rowdy on the way in."

Rachel frowned, wishing she didn't have to tell him how things had turned out. "Then you undoubtedly know what a poor price the herd commanded," she said tightly, wishing like hell she had better news to relate to him.

Travis shrugged, unconcerned. "Supply and demand. That's the way it goes."

"Thanks for the financial analysis," she countered dryly.

"Speaking of financial analyses...is that what you've been doing?" His eyes skimmed her legs and hips as he watched her get up and walk over to the file cabinet to replace a sheaf of papers.

Deciding finally she'd rather give him the news when no one else was there to witness him rub it in, she said tiredly, "I doubt I'm telling you anything you haven't already guessed, but for the record, the financial margin I thought I had is gone. I'm in the red. I haven't given up, but with the price of beef still plum-meting, I doubt there's any way I can turn things around before summer's end. Not unless I can find a buyer for the Brahma calves.''

''No luck so far?''

He didn't look as happy as Rachel would've expected him to. ''Not yet,'' Rachel said calmly. ''I do have several prospective buyers coming out to the ranch later this week. One nearly every day, as a matter of fact. That's why I was on the phone all morning.''

''Well, maybe that'll do it,'' he said.

''Maybe,'' Rachel allowed. She tried not to look too surprised at his sympathetic attitude. ''Does your showing up here mean you've decided we're friends again?'' The truth was, she had missed him terribly. Why, she didn't know. It should have been peaceful without him to badger her, but it had been lonely. She'd come to count on his disrupting presence to make her forget her troubles with the ranch and goad her into doing better, just for the pleasure of showing him she could.

Travis shrugged. ''I've made it pretty clear a simple friendship isn't what I want from you, but I'll take it over nothing any day. I've come to like having you around.''

Rachel stared at him, amazed. Realizing how open he was to compromise now, she was filled with a warm glow. Trying, however, not to let herself take his change of heart too seriously lest she get hurt in the bargain, she teased wryly, "I bet you say that to all the girls."

"No," he said softly, his eyes as serious as hers were merry. "I don't."

Their eyes held. Her mouth went dry. Rachel had the oddest feeling she was teetering on the edge. . . .

"Look, I've been thinking," Travis continued genially, plopping his Stetson down on his bent knee and idly fingering the brim. "Regardless of how all this turns out, maybe you and the kids could stay on, anyway, just live here. My mother loves the company. You could be assistant ranch manager or something."

His certainty that she would fail struck an angry chord. "Don't patronize me, Travis. And don't assume just because I haven't found a buyer for the Brahma calves thus far that I won't. I still have another month left."

"I wasn't patronizing you."

Rachel swallowed the knot of emotion in her throat. Whether he'd meant to or not, he had hurt her feelings and her pride. "The hell you weren't!" she shot back. "You're secretly glad I haven't succeeded as I'd hoped."

Travis studied her boldly. "I won't deny I expected this to happen," he began honestly, "considering your lack of ranching experience and the magnitude of the job you took on. But so what?" He shrugged as if the outcome were no big deal. "You gave it your best." He gave her a hard look. "Meant what I said earlier, about your staying on regardless of the outcome."

"No," Rachel said stiffly. Her pride wouldn't allow it.

"Why not?" His voice lowered another soothing persuasive notch. "You can't deny you like it here."

Too much. "I've already imposed enough."

"You're family, Rachel."

"Is that really the way you see me, Travis?" Rachel asked bitterly.

He drew away, alert to the anger in her gaze. "I don't know what you mean."

"I think you do."

"Well, I don't," he said tightly. "So you'll have to elaborate."

"I'd rather ask a question, instead. Are you figuring yourself into the equation?"

"In what way?" he bit back.

"Will *you* be staying on at the ranch?"

"That depends."

"On what? On whether I give in to your constant attempts at seduction and become your live-in lover?"

She'd expected him to be insulted by her cruel remarks. He only smiled, his face inscrutable. "You make it sound sordid," he said casually, getting off the desk and coming closer.

Only pride kept her from back-stepping as he approached. "That's because it is," Rachel said flatly.

He wrapped his arms around her suddenly. "That's where you're wrong, Rachel," he said softly, threading his fingers through the riot of curls at the nape of her neck. His gaze scanned her face tenderly. "Our making love could never be sordid. Enlivening. Entertaining. Fulfilling, yes. Sordid, never."

She turned away, willing him to let her go, but he didn't release her. Now they were standing, with her back to him, his arms locked about her waist, his chin in her hair.

Despite herself, Rachel almost melted into the warmth of his chest and the strength of his welcoming arms. Only the knowledge of what he really wanted from her kept her from furthering the embrace.

She uncrossed her arms and used her elbows to propel herself away from him. "I won't run around, sneak, lie or cheat," Rachel said. "I won't be with someone who's ashamed to be with me. Not again." She spun around in time to see the shock registered on Travis's face.

"Austin was ashamed of you?"

Humiliated and angry with herself for having revealed so much, she said coolly, "I never said that!"

Travis closed the distance between them swiftly and held her in front of him. "The truth, Rachel. What did my brother do?"

Rachel stared at him, her pulse racing. She'd never heard him sound so fiercely protective. "He didn't mean to do anything."

"But he did just the same, didn't he?" Travis bent his knees slightly, so he could better see into her eyes.

She turned away, irritated to find herself in the position of defending a man who had hurt her and let her down. "You don't know how hard it was for him," Rachel said, wishing she didn't feel so humiliated. "He wasn't used to dating anyone from my background."

"So?"

"So it was difficult for him, and it didn't help any that my father was usually drunk and abusive when Austin arrived to pick me up for dates." She gestured helplessly. "His friends didn't understand. Nor did his family." She paused to give Travis a pointed look that let him know how much he'd hurt her in the past. "Everyone thought he was with me for only one reason, but it wasn't true. We never made love then, although he really wanted to—" Again, realizing she had said far too much, she stopped speaking abruptly.

"Is that why he married you? Because you refused to put out?"

Rachel sighed miserably, taking no offense because none was meant. "In retrospect, I think that probably was part of it. And I think subconsciously he wanted to get back at your father for putting so much pressure on him to run the ranch."

He studied her quietly. "And you, Rachel? What about you?" he asked softly. "What were you thinking?"

Rachel figured she'd been foolishly honest so far. She might as well tell him the rest. "I knew I came from an ill-thought-of home. I wasn't going to be labeled a tramp, too."

"But to actually marry someone, Rachel, to commit to them for life..." Travis said, aghast.

"You have to understand," she said, her humiliation fading as she saw the understanding in his eyes. "We may have had very different views about the nature and course of our relationship, but we also thought we were very much in love. We were both so young, Travis, and so very naive. We really thought we could make it work. We thought getting married would legitimize our relationship, make it more acceptable to family and community."

"But it had just the opposite effect," Travis recalled sadly.

"Yes. Everyone resented me even more."

"Including Austin?"

Rachel knew there was no point in denying it and she nodded. "Yes," she said simply. "He was hurt when his family wouldn't accept our relationship and hurt when my father didn't even seem to care what happened to me. And I think, whether he meant to or not, that deep inside he blamed me for all of it."

Travis was silent for a long time. "I don't see what any of that has to do with us," he said finally.

"I won't hurt your mother that way. And I won't set a poor example for my teenage children."

"My mother wants us to get together."

"She wants us to declare a truce and be friends," Rachel corrected. "That's not the same thing."

"It could be," he said quietly.

"No, Travis."

Silence fell between them. He looked at her tenderly. She had the oddest impression that at that moment he would have a hard time denying her anything. She knew she wanted to please him, as well, to win his approval and his understanding, if only for the sake of knowing she had done it.

"I still want you, Rachel," he said quietly.

And I still want you. But she also knew their circumstances were far too complicated ever to let a love between them flourish. Travis knew it, too. Otherwise, he'd be talking permanent relationship, not temporary love affair.

Her eyes still riveted to his, she shook her head sadly. "I won't be your mistress, Travis." The edges of her mouth curved up in a bitter smile. "Not even if doing so allowed me to continue on as assistant manager of this ranch. And that's final."

"It's so GOOD to be home!" Jaclyn said a mere four hours later.

"It's so good to have you all home again!" Rachel said, embracing all three weary travelers in turn. *And not to be alone with Travis anymore.*

Every time she looked at him, she heard his low sexy voice ringing in her ear. *I still want you, Rachel.*

But sex wasn't just a physical act to her, like brushing her teeth or working out. It was a commitment to each other and to the future, a blending of heart and soul. To Travis it was apparently just something pleasurable.

Dinner that evening was lively. The twins looked tanned and healthy, content to be back on the ranch again, as was Jaclyn. Travis looked happy, too.

"It sounds like you did everything there was to do in Florida," Rachel marveled.

"Just about," Gretchen said. "But we would've had a better time if we hadn't been so worried about you. It wasn't right that we got to take a super vacation and you had to stay here all alone and work."

"She wasn't alone," Brett put in with a yawn. "Uncle Travis was here."

"Speaking of work," Rachel added lightly. "I've got some chores in mind for the two of you this week, starting tomorrow."

The twins groaned in unison. "We hate ranch work," Brett complained.

"Too bad, 'cause you're going to do it, anyway. Besides, it builds character." Rachel grinned.

Surveying the twins with a mixture of maternal pride and exasperation, Rachel wondered if they ever would appreciate all she was doing for them this summer, working her fingers to the bone, just so they would have a secure future. Not that it really mattered. She was going to take care of them, whether they appreciated her efforts or not.

Jaclyn sent a curious look at her son. "How did the two of you get along without us?"

"Fine." Travis smiled at his mother innocently, then turned to her. "Isn't that right, Rachel?"

Depends on what you meant by fine, Rachel thought. If he meant that she was supposed to have been in a perpetual state of excitement, they'd gotten along tremendously. Rachel smiled. "We managed just fine."

Jaclyn looked from Rachel to Travis. There was no masking either the speculation or disappointment in her eyes. Clearly, she'd been hoping for so much more to develop.

Chapter Twelve

"Mix that crazy cow back in with the herd? Are you loco?" Rowdy said incredulously the following morning.

Rachel sat back calmly in her office chair. "That's what I said, Rowdy."

Rowdy looked at the only other person in the room for help. "Travis, tell her she's crazy."

Travis looked up from the copier in Rachel's office, where he was copying a sheaf of papers relating to his airline business. He sent Rachel an ornery grin and parroted, "You're crazy."

Rachel swiveled around to face him. She wished Travis would quit wearing that tantalizing cologne of his. Every time she caught a whiff of sandalwood and spice, she was reminded of the night by the windmill and how it had felt to be so thoroughly, wickedly, close to him. She returned his parody of a grin. "Thanks ever so much, but you have nothing to do with this, Travis."

Travis picked up his papers and swaggered toward her, his hips undulating in a smooth male motion. He deposited his papers on a corner of her desk and sat down in a chair next to Rowdy. He slouched low on his spine, propped his elbows on the chair arms and templed his fingers above the midpoint of his chest. "Why do you want to move the steer, anyway?"

"Because I need that corral next to the barns," Rachel said.

"What for?" Rowdy asked.

"I'm planning to put the organic herd there."

Both Rowdy and Travis did double takes. "All fifty?" they said in unison.

The force of their incredulity sent a blush of warmth to her cheeks that made the blusher she'd put on that morning quite unnecessary. "Just for the day," Rachel qualified. Because they were still both looking at her as though she was from outer space, she continued conversationally, "A prospective buyer is coming out to look at the herd. Which reminds me, Rowdy, as soon as you're done moving the steer, bring all the men to the barn."

Rowdy stood in anticipation of being dismissed, holding his hat in front of his knees. "How come?"

"We're going to groom those calves and give them baths."

Rowdy squinted at her. Rachel refused to even look at Travis.

"You're kidding, right?" Rowdy asked. Beside him Travis remained ominously silent.

"No," Rachel told her cow boss calmly. She looked directly at Rowdy and didn't drop her gaze. "I want those calves looking like they're ready to win a blue ribbon at the county fair."

"Now hold on there, Rachel," Travis said, leaning forward in his chair. "This isn't a 4-H project—"

"You're right. It isn't." Rachel smiled at her cow boss. "Rowdy, you're excused."

The foreman shook his head glumly, plopped his Stetson on his head and turned to leave. "Keep trying to talk some sense into her, Travis," he muttered on his way out in a voice Rachel knew only Travis was meant to hear. Rowdy sent Travis a brief man-to-man glance. "God knows I can't."

Rowdy left. Travis turned back to Rachel. From the way he looked at her, she knew she was in for a fight.

"I gotta agree with him. This is the dumbest thing you've ever done, assigning the hands to play beauty parlor to a bunch of calves." He stood and moved forward to sit on a corner of her desk.

Rachel's heart pounded at his nearness. He had shaved very closely that morning. His gleaming black hair was agreeably mussed.

"It's not as if I'm going to make them do this every day, Travis. Besides," she continued confidently, "they'll be singing a different tune when I cut the deal with Rob McMillan."

Travis blinked in surprise and fastened his eyes on her like twin lasers. "Who's he?"

"Only the owner of the biggest chain of natural-food stores in the Midwest." Finding the intensity of his gaze as disconcerting as the washboard flatness of his abdomen and the bunched muscles beneath his shirt, Rachel got up to pour herself some coffee from a silver service.

Travis followed her. He picked up a teacup from the tray, frowned at the delicate china pattern, then poured himself some coffee, too. "Then he probably already has a line of organically raised beef," Travis countered.

Rachel smiled and took a seat on the sofa. "Nope. He doesn't. Until now, Rob's only carried fish and poultry in his stores. But he's thinking of getting into organically raised beef."

Travis frowned again. He swallowed his coffee in a single gulp. Avoiding her eyes, he put his cup aside. "Where'd you hear that?"

"The last Southwestern Cattle Raisers Association meeting," Rachel said, then added confidently, "and Travis? I intend to be that supplier."

TRAVIS HAD TO ADMIRE her determination, even if he did think she was going overboard. And he wasn't the only one who shared that opinion.

"Come on, Uncle Travis," the twins complained after lunch as they hauled buckets of sudsy water over to the seventy-five-pound calves. "Get us out of this."

Travis laughed at the twins' aversion to physical labor, remembering he himself had felt exactly the same

way at that age. "No can do. Your mama is determined to have every one of those fifty calves washed,
rinsed and blow-dried." Even if it was the craziest
thing he'd ever heard.

"Towel-dried," Rachel corrected, tossing Brett a
towel so he could rub down a just-scrubbed animal
and lead him to the pen. "And it'd go a lot faster if
you'd lend a hand, Travis."

"Yeah, Uncle Travis. If we have to wash these baby
cows, you should, too," Gretchen persisted, her hands
on her hips.

"One for all and all for one," Brett continued persuasively.

Watching the twins band together and back each
other up, Travis was reminded of the camaraderie he'd
shared with Austin when they were kids. Now, with
Austin's children on the ranch, he felt a sense of family that had been lacking in his life for a long time.
And the twins, though clearly no ranchers, seemed to
be enjoying living here, too. As far as his mother went,
she was in seventh heaven. Not a day went by that she
didn't plan and execute some special activity for or
with her grandchildren.

"Unless, of course..." Rachel paused archly, refusing to finish her sentence.

Travis couldn't resist when she looked at him that
flirtatiously. He edged nearer and captured the other
end of the towel she held in her hand. "What?"

Using the towel they were both holding as leverage, she pulled him aside and teased, "You're afraid to get really down and dirty with the rest of us."

He saw the challenge in her eyes, then picked up the water hose, pressed the trigger release on the nozzle and squirted her in the middle. "Watch who you're calling squeamish, Miss Rachel."

Rachel squealed as the spray of cold water hit her. She tossed a soapy sponge. It bounced off his shoulder. Bubbles splashed into his face.

"Okay, that does it," Travis said. "Now you've declared war." He retrieved the sponge from the grass, dunked it in the bucket and lobbed it at her nose. She ducked at the last minute.

"Ugh!" She straightened, hands on her hips. Her face was bright red with embarrassment. Travis thought he'd never seen her look prettier.

"Kill him, Mom!" Brett yelled encouragement from the sidelines as the hands turned around to watch.

"Yeah. Get him good!" Gretchen said. "Don't let him get away with that."

Her beautiful lips pursed with anything but amusement. "No," she said primly, turning her back on him. "I don't think I will."

The corral was dead silent as Rachel walked back to her bucket and picked up the sponge and the hose. Soapy sponge in one hand, hose in the other, she turned toward a calf. Travis's spirits sagged. What he'd hoped would be a little bit of horseplay had somehow turned into a fight. He gave the twins a guess-we-better-get-back-to-work shrug and turned to locate a sponge.

He'd just bent down to retrieve one, when the water hit him square in the seat of the pants. She had a good aim. He ran toward her, swearing revenge.

Laughing, Rachel backed up and tried to dodge his advance. With a whoop and a holler, Travis wrested the hose from her hands. Or at least tried to, but she held on tight. Before he knew it the trigger nozzle had been pressed down, and they ended up squirting Rowdy.

Rowdy, who was no slouch in the water-fight department, promptly got the both of them back with *his* hose. Gretchen, Brett and the rest of the hands joined in the fun. Soon sponges were flying and hoses were being squirted in every direction. Laughter and shouting and good-natured ribbing filled the air.

It was at least half an hour before anyone got back to work.

"IMPRESSIVE, AREN'T THEY?" Rachel murmured hours later as she and Travis stood alone, admiring the calves in the newly sodded pen.

She was impressive, Travis thought, with her sunburned nose and her crazy ideas and the way she'd cheerfully organized everyone and gotten the job done. "I gotta admit they do look...better," Travis said.

"Admit it, Travis." She nudged his leg playfully with one of hers. "They looked darned good."

"Like pampered pets." He stood shoulder to shoulder with her at the corral, his foot propped up on the bottom rail of the fence. "But I'm not so sure that's the image you're going for, Rachel."

"It's exactly the image I'm going for." Rachel turned toward him earnestly.

Travis had wanted to kiss her all afternoon. The presence of the hired hands and the kids had prevented it during the water fight. The fact they were in such a public place and it was still broad daylight prevented it even now. But it wouldn't prevent it forever. Because Travis knew he *was* going to kiss her again.

"Trust me, Rob McMillan is going to love it," Rachel continued cheerfully.

Rob McMillan is going to love you, Travis thought.

His good mood souring fast, Travis demanded, "What do you know about this guy, anyway? Have you ever met him?"

Rachel gazed adoringly out at her scrawny spanking-clean Brahma calves, who at this point in their development were not much bigger than large dogs. "Not face-to-face," she admitted. "But I've talked to him on the phone at length."

"Is he young?" Travis asked.

Rachel turned toward him, her golden eyes filled with a suspicious light. "Why?"

Travis shrugged. "I don't know. I just wondered."

"Well, he's young," Rachel replied with a mixture of smugness and resentment as she turned back to her herd. "And single. A real go-getter."

Travis felt his jaw set. "Hopefully, you'll get what you want from the meeting." *A deal on your calves so you'll have more time to spend with me.* Now where had that thought come from? he wondered, perplexed.

"Thanks. I hope it goes well, too." She smiled at him, looking relaxed again and happy to be with him. Suddenly she gave a little gasp. It was remarkably similar to the soft womanly sounds she made during sex, Travis realized uncomfortably. She glanced at her watch.

"Gosh it's late," Rachel murmured. "Rob will be here soon." Glancing down at her damp jeans and stained shirt, she shook her head ruefully. "I better get cleaned up."

And I'd like to help, Travis thought, easily able to imagine the two of them in a hot steamy shower. "It probably wouldn't hurt to put on a dry pair of jeans."

Rachel laughed softly and sent him a mute reproving glance. "Don't be silly. I'm going to wear a dress."

IT HAD BEEN such a nice day, Rachel thought, as she reclined in the fragrant bubble bath. It hadn't started out that way, of course, with the men grumbling and carrying on. But when the twins had come out to help and Travis had joined in, it had been great. For the first time since she'd been living at the ranch, she'd felt as though she and Travis were connected by more than just the past and the Westcott name. And wrong or not, she would have liked the day to end with her wrapped in his arms.

Closing her eyes, she could easily envision many more days like today. Meals together. Holidays. She could see them playing, fighting, loving and living together, day after wonderful day. But that was fantasy, not reality, she told herself firmly. Travis wasn't interested in running the ranch with her. Or in working by her side. Or in having a family.

So what if they were no longer sworn enemies and were on the verge of being trusted friends? So what if she was still wildly attracted to him and he made love to her the way no other man ever could or would? He was completely charming, disarming, hardworking and successful, but that didn't make him any more marriageable, or an intimate relationship between them any more possible.

Travis was an emotional drifter. He wanted a woman who would love him physically without attaching any emotional strings. As much as Rachel appreciated the exultant abandon of his kisses, the thoroughly satisfied way he had made her feel when he'd made love to her, she could never be with him again. Not knowing he was still as footloose as he had ever been when it came to the women in his life.

She might be able to do without a ring on her finger, if she knew Travis really loved her, and only her. But she couldn't do without commitment. If she was to be with him again, he would have to pledge his heart and soul to her first. He would have to promise her tomorrow, not just today.

TRAVIS HADN'T MEANT to bother Rachel when she was getting ready to greet a guest, but he couldn't help but stop and gape when he passed by the open doorway to her bedroom. He hadn't seen her look so dressed up and pretty since that night the previous spring when he'd first seen her again. The navy blue denim shirt-dress she was wearing looked brand-new and fit her willowy body with unerring sensual accuracy. The bodice snugly hugged her breasts. A wide silver belt drew attention to her slender waist. Beneath the hem of the full skirt he could see the frilly edge of a white lace petticoat and was irritated to see she'd left the bottom two buttons of the skirt undone to further show it off, just as she had left the top two buttons undone.

"You look like you're ready to go on a date, not to a business meeting," Travis remarked, watching as Rachel bent to slip her stocking-clad feet into her dressy cowboy boots, which had been polished to a shine.

"Good." Rachel sighed, satisfied. "Because that's sort of what we're doing."

"What?"

"We're going to dinner in San Angelo as soon as Rob's toured the ranch and seen the herd. I've arranged to have some of our nonorganic Westcott beef prepared for us by one of the chefs in his hotel restaurant. Wasn't that clever of me?''

"Stunningly clever," Travis said dryly, all too aware it *was* a good move on her part. The beef they raised on the ranch was of superior quality. "I still think..."

"What?" Rachel paused in the act of fastening silver hoop earrings in her ears.

You should button up that dress. "Are you sure you shouldn't wear a suit?" Travis asked. *Something not quite so sexy or feminine or flirty.*

"Well, actually, I thought about it," Rachel admitted conversationally as she ran a brush expertly through her springy flame-colored curls. "But I really want to look like a lady rancher, you know?" She put down the brush and used her fingertips to fluff up the ends of her hair. "And maybe it's corny, but this is what I think I should wear. After all, we're selling Texas and the traditions of the Old West, so a Western-style dress seemed perfect."

She spritzed on some delicious-smelling perfume, then paused and looked concerned. "Why? You don't think... I don't look fat in this dress, do I?" Hands on her hips, she rushed to the full-length mirror and pirouetted slowly.

"No." The problem was she looked too beautiful. Travis tried not to groan as she smoothed the fabric of her skirt over her slender hips with the palms of her hands. "No, you don't look fat." He strolled close to her.

"Then what is it?" Perplexed, Rachel whirled to face him.

I'm jealous as hell, that's what's the matter, and I know I have no right to be. No right at all. "Nothing." His desire for her was his problem, and it was something he was just going to have to deal with.

The sound of a car sliced through the silence.

"Oh, my gosh!" Rachel dashed to the window just as a sleek stretch limousine pulled up in front of the house. "He's here!" She raced past Travis, pausing only long enough to give him a quick sisterly kiss on the cheek. "Wish me luck!" she cried excitedly.

With the business deal, Travis wished her all the luck in the world. But not with Rob McMillan personally.

"WHEN WILL YOU LET me know?" Rachel asked as their coffee cups were cleared away.

The handsome entrepreneur grinned at her. Blond, blue-eyed and suntanned, he looked like a California surfer. In the past, she would have been immediately attracted. Now, Rachel realized sadly, in the romance department, he couldn't so much as ignite a match. Romance for her involved tall Texans with black hair, slate-blue eyes and smart oh-so-sensual mouths. Romance for her was filled with as much heartache as it was impossibility. But Travis was the only man who interested her, even if he was all wrong for her.

"I've got a few other avenues to check out first," Rob was saying.

"I understand." Rachel smiled, encouraged by the rapport they'd established. She gathered up the projected figures and reports she had prepared for Rob, handed him his copies and stuck her copies back in her briefcase. "I try to be thorough, too."

"But I'll try and let you know by the end of the month," he promised. "So, now that we've concluded our business, want to go dancing?"

Rachel smiled and thought of Travis back at the ranch waiting for her, curious to know how things had gone. "Thanks," she said pleasantly. "But it's been a long day."

"I understand." Rob stood chivalrously as Rachel gathered her purse and briefcase. "I'll call you with my decision."

Rachel shook his hand firmly and looked square into his eyes. "I'll look forward to hearing from you."

Their goodbyes said, she started for the exit. She was nearly to the door when she saw him, sitting at the end of the bar, nursing what looked to be an untouched beer and a bowl of pretzels.

She sauntered to his side. She grinned, admitting to herself that in his tweed blazer and hat, Travis had never looked sexier. Or more Texan. "Fancy meeting you here," she said.

"Yeah, well, I worried about your getting home all right. Since you rode into town in Barry's limousine and all."

"It's Rob, as in Robert, not Barry. And I planned to take a cab." She softened, oddly touched. "Did you have dinner?"

"No." He slapped a bill onto the counter and stood. He grinned. "I was too busy watching you eat." He took her arm, and by unspoken agreement, they headed out of the restaurant. "So, how was the Westcott beef?"

"Delicious," Rachel said. Yet she couldn't help but think it would have tasted even better had she been sharing the meal with Travis, instead of Rob. "How come you didn't come and join us?

He looked down at her as if she was the most fascinating woman in the world. "I didn't want to intrude," he said softly.

Rachel's tummy did a little flip-flop. "Just making sure I made it home okay?"

"Mothers," Travis lamented, then shrugged as if it was all Jaclyn's fault. "Mine instilled me with manners."

"I've never had a bodyguard before," she drawled, as together they stepped out into the warm Texas night.

Travis paused and just gazed at her. The seconds ticked by. As she stared up at him, Rachel realized that the animosity between them was completely gone. They still might disagree, and heatedly when they differed in ideology, but they no longer mistrusted one another.

"How does it feel having a bodyguard?" he asked softly.

Rachel held his gaze. It had been a long time since she'd been protected by a man. And she knew Travis's devotion was something she could not only manage to get used to, but something she was beginning to covet. "Good," she almost whispered. "Damn good."

"WAS YOUR DAY as hectic as mine?"

"Change that to the last several days, and the answer is yes," Rachel replied as Travis joined her in the kitchen. In fact, they'd both been so busy they hadn't really seen each other since he'd brought her home from San Angelo.

"Everyone else asleep?" Travis asked.

"Everyone except the two of us." Rachel brought a tin of cookies and a carton of milk to the kitchen table. "It's after midnight."

Travis found two glasses and sat down opposite her. It was funny, he thought. Women had come and gone in his life over the years. But with Rachel it was different. More and more these days, his moods were directly linked to her. When they fought, his thoughts were black as thunder. When she smiled at him, he knew a new kind of peace. A new kind of want. One that just wouldn't go away.

"I know why I'm still up." She smiled and turned her golden-brown eyes on him. She poured herself a glass of milk. "I'm wired, because I met with another prospective buyer for the Brahma herd."

Travis took a cookie from the tin and snapped it in two. "How'd it go?"

"Great." Rachel kicked back in her chair. "I know I said the same thing after I met with Rob McMillan, but I think I really might have a buyer this time."

"Bathing the cows really helped, huh?"

She wrinkled her nose at him. "You're making fun of me," she accused.

"Sure am," he admitted with a wink. "How much grumbling did the hands do this time?"

"Just as much as the twins, as usual," Rachel reported. "I didn't care. I still don't." She sat forward earnestly. "I know sprucing those Brahma calves up makes a difference."

Women! "If you say so."

"You're making fun of me again."

"Yep."

They grinned at each other.

"How's *your* business going?" she asked.

"Like gangbusters, at the moment," Travis said. "Our summer ticket sales exceeded all expectations. That's where I was today—in Fort Worth, meeting with my staff, trying to determine the travel dates for the special rates next year."

"Is it hard for you, working out of the ranch?"

"Actually it doesn't seem to make much difference," Travis admitted. "Anyway, I know the business so well now I could run it with my eyes closed."

It was himself that was the problem. Lately everything he'd thought he knew about himself seemed wrong. He'd figured ranching wasn't his passion. Yet he couldn't bear to let the Bar W go to Rachel or anyone else. He'd also been dead certain he would never marry. Now, knowing marriage was what Rachel wanted out of life, he found himself thinking about it, too. In the abstract, anyway.

Struggling to keep his mind on their conversation, instead of on how well her Western dress outlined her breasts when she sat back in her chair that way, he asked casually, "Was your prospective buyer impressed with the ranch?"

"Of course. Who wouldn't be?"

"You really feel it's impressive?"

She held his gaze. "Don't you?"

He nodded, feeling more content than he had in a long time. And it was all because of her. It was hard to remember why he had once resented her. Impossible to stop thinking about one day making love with her again. Even though she kept telling him it would never happen...

"In the years I was away," Rachel confided as she got up to look out the kitchen window, "I used to dream of this place. The way it was when I was a kid."

She turned to face him, her hands braced against the windowsill. Travis joined her at the window and glanced out at the grounds. "Were they happy dreams?" *Were they about Austin?*

"Sometimes. Sometimes not. I envied you so much," she whispered.

"Why?"

"For having grown up here and been part of such a respected family in the community."

"It wasn't that different," Travis asserted.

"Wasn't it?"

His gaze roved over her flowing hair and fair skin. A little too much sun had just colored her nose and cheeks.

"I would've given anything to have this kind of security," Rachel continued. "In my case, appearances were not deceiving," she confirmed sadly. "Like I've said, my father either drank or gambled away everything he made."

"What about when the twins were born?"

She shrugged and, pushing away from the window, strolled about the kitchen. "There's still a great deal of difference between the life we had in Beaumont and this. So much that sometimes I worry about corrupting the twins."

He followed her. "And at other times?"

"I want to give them permanent financial security. Maybe it's selfish of me in a way, but it's what I want."

Why couldn't it be like this between them all the time? he wondered. So open and honest. "It's not selfish to want to take care of your children, Rachel," he assured her. "That's why I asked you to consider staying on at summer's end."

"And I told you," she said firmly, tightening her lips in prim disapproval, "I can't do that."

His impatience had him tensing. "Why not?"

She sent him a level look, her mood just as intractable as his. "You know why."

Yeah, Travis thought, he did. But it had nothing to do with finances or the deal with his mother or even her past with his brother and their former animosity, as she would have him believe. It had to do with her feelings, and his, and the fact that neither of them could seem to control them for long, not when they were together. But Rachel still wouldn't face that. The evasion in her eyes now prompted him to act.

"Because of this?" he asked matter-of-factly. He hauled her into his arms and kissed her senseless, until she was trembling, until she was kissing him back, wrapping her arms around his neck and holding him close, her body soft and warm and pliant against the length in his. He threaded his hands through the tangle of curls at her neck and tilted her head back. "That's not a reason to leave, Rachel. That's a reason to stay."

Chapter Thirteen

"Look, Mom, I think it's great that you want to run the ranch, but Gretchen and I don't ever want to run it. So, if that's where this talk is leading..." Brett said as he and Gretchen joined her in her office for a family powwow.

Rachel looked at their faces and thought about how much they looked like their father. And Travis, too. Whether the twins realized it or not, this ranch was not just a link to their past and their father. It was a part of them. "I thought you liked living here," she said.

"We do. We love it. We love Gran and Uncle Travis, too.

"But that doesn't change our plans for the future," Brett continued. "We still want to go to college. And we're not studying agriculture," Brett continued firmly, reading Rachel's mind. "I want to study filmmaking. Gretchen wants to major in fashion design."

Rachel stared at her children in bewilderment. "This ranch is your legacy from your father," she said. "It's your connection to him."

"Maybe so. But does that mean we have to run it?" Brett complained.

"I think that's what Gran wants," Gretchen interjected practically, her expression glum.

"Well, couldn't we just let you run the ranch, since you like it so much?" Brett asked Rachel hopefully. "And when you get too old—"

"Banish the thought, young man!" Rachel corrected with a loving smile.

Brett grinned. "Well, you can hire someone else to do it."

"Yeah, or train one of *our* kids when we have them," Gretchen added.

Rachel sighed. How could her children not want what she was working so hard to attain for them? "I suppose there's a chance you'll change your mind," she said.

"Don't hold your breath," Brett advised with his customary candor. "But I don't mind *you* running the ranch. In fact we both like it, 'cause we see more of you this way."

That was true, Rachel knew. Working out of an office at home made her instantly accessible.

"So what's up?" Travis said, coming in just as the twins left.

"Brett and Gretchen have told me, as much as they love living here, that neither of them want anything to do with running the ranch."

Travis went to the window. He stood with his back to her, his hands shoved in the pockets of his jeans. "Then why break your back doing it for them?"

"Because I like doing it," Rachel said. "And because they might change their minds."

He shot her an arch look over his shoulder. "From hints I've picked up, I'd say that's doubtful."

She bristled. "Children don't always know what's best for them."

He turned and leaned against the window. "But they have the right to choose their own paths in life."

"Yes, they do," Rachel agreed. She met his glance levelly. "And I would never force them to manage the ranch against their will. I will, however, work diligently to protect their investment. And the income from the ranch will allow them to pursue their dreams, whatever they are."

"Aren't you leaving something out?" He started for her, his strides long and lazy.

"Like what?" Rachel asked, her heart pounding. His closeness was overwhelming. She liked it when they talked intimately about themselves to each other. And yet it was difficult for her, because every time they did, she wound up yearning to be held in his arms again.

"Like the fact that you want this ranch for yourself," Travis said in a flat noncommittal tone.

She flushed at his blunt unexpected attack. "It's not that simple, Travis."

Travis fell silent, but she knew from the way he looked at her that he disagreed. To him, it was simple. The ranch had always been his. Now she was trying her very best to take it away from him, not just on a temporary basis but for all time.

Rachel sighed. She hated the position Jaclyn had put her in. But prior to Rachel's appearance, Travis had rarely been out at the ranch. If she left, Rachel was willing to bet Travis would go straight back to Fort Worth. Rowdy would run the ranch, and it would no longer be cared for on a day-to-day basis by family.

She studied Travis, loving the suntanned hue of his face and the laugh lines that feathered out around his eyes. "Are you angry with me?"

He shrugged, shoved a hand through the tousled layers of his glossy black hair and said gruffly, "At the moment I don't know how I feel."

One minute he loved her. The next he resented her. Yet through it all she remained constantly on his mind. Rachel was the first thing he thought of every morning, and the last thing he thought of before he went to sleep. Hell, these days, he even dreamed about her. He could no longer imagine the ranch without her. And yet, something in him still rankled at the enormity of what both she and his mother were asking him to give up.

"As much as I wanted to earn the right to run this ranch, I never wanted to take anything from you," Rachel persisted, her golden eyes on his.

"But you have, anyway," Travis countered quietly, his feelings an ambivalent mix as he regarded her gravely. "That's the hell of it, Rachel." His voice dropped a weary notch. "You have, anyway."

Travis was halfway out the door when the phone rang. Rachel picked it up on the first ring, while Travis lingered in the doorway, waiting to see if the call was for him.

"Yes, Sheriff," Rachel said. She listened intently, her expression growing grimmer and more troubled with every second. "I apologize for the inconvenience. Yes. I promise I'll take care of it right away. I'll see to it personally," she promised, then said a swift goodbye.

Travis started for her. As he did so, he realized how much his feelings had changed. Two months ago, he would have relished any calamity Rachel faced. Now he wanted only to protect her. "Bad news?"

Rachel was already reaching for her hat. "We've got cows out on the highway."

"Which means we've got fence down somewhere, too. Who's available to help?"

"No one except you and me."

She slipped on her flat-brimmed hat and pushed the string tie up to her throat to secure it. Her eyes lifted to his. Travis thought he'd never seen her looking so pretty. Or determined to succeed.

"Will you help?" she asked.

Suddenly, who owned the ranch didn't matter. Travis just knew he couldn't let her down. His hand flat on the small of her back, he propelled her through the door. "How's your lassoing coming?" he teased.

Rachel grinned and winked up at him. "Guess we'll find out, won't we, cowboy?"

As it turned out, there were only three cows on the highway, and Rachel and Travis were easily able to herd them back to Westcott land. As they approached the pasture, the going got rougher. Travis swore. "I count twelve, no, fifteen more outside the fence."

"Looks like we've got our work cut out for us," Rachel said grimly. As they approached on horseback, the cows scattered and began to run. Rachel went wide to the left, Travis wide to the right.

As she worked her horse back and forth, most of the cows settled down and went obediently back to the middle, toward the fence. All except one. Frisky and mulish, he tried to outrun her. Rachel picked up her lasso and swung. She missed her target the first time. But not the second. She reeled him in as Travis finished herding the rest of the strays back into the pasture.

"Nice work," he said when Rachel caught up with him. "You've really improved with that lasso."

"You can probably credit my teacher with that," she remarked.

"Oh?"

Her hands on the saddle horn, she shifted forward in the saddle and regarded him with mock seriousness. "He said I was swinging my lasso too low," she confided. "He was right."

Travis thought about how she had transformed herself from city slicker to rancher extraordinaire by sheer grit and a desire to succeed. The resentment he'd been feeling toward her fled completely. He was foolish to resent her for wanting the ranch, because she cared about it in a way he hadn't for years and probably never would again.

His eyes locked with hers as he tugged the brim of his hat lower. "I imagine you taught that teacher of yours a thing or two, as well," Travis said softly.

I hope so, Rachel thought.

And suddenly Travis saw her not taking something he loved from him, but giving him his freedom. It was days just like today that he had always dreaded. Now, he no longer had to deal with inevitable ranch calamities. His first love was still the Texas-based commuter airline he'd started from scratch and turned into a multimillion-dollar business.

He started to tell her about his change of heart, but the air filled with earsplitting bleating. Rachel and

Travis turned in unison. A calf had gotten tangled in the downed barbed wire. Two more cows were heading for the fence opening. "Never a dull moment," Rachel murmured. Already swinging herself out of the saddle and down to the ground, she said, "You head off those would-be strays and get the fence back up. I'll get the calf."

"Gotcha." Travis touched two fingers to the brim of his hat and grinned at her. She grinned back at him as he prodded his horse's belly with his heels and took off.

"Come on, baby. Hang on. I'll get you out." Speaking in musical soothing tones, Rachel grabbed the calf around the throat with one arm and straddled his back. Subduing him with her weight, she began to pry the wire from the calf's legs. Then, maintaining the pressure around his throat, she backed the calf away from the offending wire.

"How bad's he hurt?" Travis asked, returning and climbing down from his horse.

Rachel inspected the deep jagged lacerations. "These wounds need to be cleansed and bandaged." Still holding the calf between her legs, Rachel took her scarf off and ripped it in half.

Travis nodded grimly, apparently agreeing with her. "I'll finish the fence. Then we'll head back."

"We're taking this calf with us," Rachel called after his retreating back. She bent over to secure a makeshift bandage. The calf bawled hysterically when she touched him. Startled by the ferocity of the sound, Rachel jumped and backed into another cow, who was grazing nearby. The injured calf bawled again, and without warning the whole herd became excited and took up the complaint. Cows began to scatter every which way, mooing and knocking into one another in their haste.

Rachel struggled to hold on to the calf just long enough to secure another bandage.

"Rachel, watch out!" Travis shouted.

She lifted her head, saw him drop his tools and head for her at a run. At the naked fear on Travis's face, she sucked in an uneven breath. She turned and saw a steer charging at her, his eyes huge and wild. Only it wasn't just any steer. It was the same one that had attacked Bobby Ray. She screamed and dodged. The next thing she knew, the animal had ducked his head and sent another cow flying into the barbed-wired fence Travis had just strung tight. It crashed down under the weight of the cow.

The steer turned around again, a crazed look in his eyes, and took off again, charging wildly down the field into the center of the now stampeding cows. Knowing she had to subdue him, Rachel jumped on her horse and followed him.

She raised her rope above her head, aimed and threw.

She caught him squarely around the neck and tightened the noose. He skidded to a halt, as Rachel's horse closed the distance between them. And it was then, as Rachel came right up on him that the crazed cow jerked like a bucking bronco and took off again, pulling Rachel right along with him.

"Let him go, dammit!" Travis shouted from somewhere behind her, but Rachel held on stubbornly, her horse cutting in and out of the herd of excited cattle. She continued to hold tight even as she was jerked from the saddle and pulled along the ground. Finally the steer ran out of air and collapsed on his haunches in the dust.

Travis rode up, leapt out of his saddle and hunkered down beside her. Around them, the stampede had quieted. The day had been saved.

"Rachel," Travis said, his voice sounding strange and shaky. "Oh, God...Rachel," he whispered. "You're hurt."

"I am?" Rachel asked, dazed. She put her hand to her aching forehead, and when she took it away it was covered in blood.

"YOU CAN SEE HER NOW, Mr. Westcott," the nurse in Emergency said.

Travis sprang to his feet. It had been forty-five minutes since he'd brought Rachel in, but it seemed like days.

He found her lying on a gurney, a sheet drawn up to her chest. Her skin looked as pale as the hospital gown she was wearing. Resisting the urge to haul her into his arms and smother her face with kisses, Travis took her trembling hand in his. She looked so vulnerable it tore at his heart. He hated seeing her this way. And yet he had never been prouder of her than when she had lassoed that crazy cow.

"I had to have a tetanus shot," she complained. "How do you like the bandage?" She forced a weak smile and used her free hand to point to her temple.

"Cute."

"The doctor says it's so close to my hairline the scar'll never show."

"No concussion?" Travis scanned her face worriedly.

She shook her head, then winced, as if in pain. "No. Just a headache from where I was stitched up."

"I thought they numbed you before they started sewing."

"They did. It still hurts." She released a wavering breath and held his hand tightly. "Did you get hold of Rowdy?"

"Sure did. They're finishing the job we started."

"At least they didn't have to tend to that crazy cow."

"No, they didn't. Thanks to your lassoing skill."

"And the way you tied him up," Rachel added.

"He was out of commission. So everything's back to normal now," Travis reassured her. "And they took that little calf that got tangled up in the barbed wire to the vet, too."

"Oh, Travis, I'm so sorry this happened," Rachel whispered.

"You've got nothing to be sorry about. No one could have subdued that steer faster or more expertly than you did, and that includes me."

"But it was all my fault. I never should have instructed Rowdy to mix him back in with the herd."

"You don't have to talk about this now if it's going to upset you," he declared huskily, figuring if *she* cried *he'd* end up crying and embarrassing them both.

"No." Rachel's lips quavered and she lifted her golden eyes to his. "I want to talk about it, Travis. I want you to know if I'd had any idea how vicious that cow could really be, I would have ordered him destroyed. You were right. It wasn't worth the liability to keep him."

Travis sat down beside her on the hospital gurney. "I wish I hadn't been right," he said softly. His eyes searched hers, making sure for the hundredth time since she'd taken the spill from her horse that she really was all right. "I never wanted to see you hurt."

"I know." Her hand softened beneath his, becoming pliant and acquiescent, just as her mouth, her whole body had, when they'd made love. "How did you know something like this would happen?"

He shrugged, wishing he could be with her like this and not desire her, wishing he could stop wanting to protect her or stop feeling as if she was his top priority now and to hell with the ranch. To hell with everything except her.

"Years of experience," he answered her quietly. "What Rowdy and Bobby Ray said was true. Some cows, like people, are just plain mean and ornery."

They were silent. "Well, next time I'll know better," Rachel said firmly as she pulled herself together. "Next time I'll listen to you and Rowdy when you try to tell me something."

Travis smoothed the tangled auburn curls from her face and smiled at her.

"What's so funny?"

Travis shrugged again. "I was just thinking. When you first came, I wanted nothing more than to be able to tell you what to do and have you do it. Now that you're actually listening to me, though, I wonder if maybe I didn't like you better the other way. You know, kind of feisty and temperamental—"

She aimed a teasing blow at his shoulder.

He caught her fist and unthinkingly pressed a kiss into her knuckles."

"Oh, Travis," she sighed, "are we ever going to come to terms with our situation?"

Travis smiled at her. "I think I already have."

"What do you mean?"

"It's not the ranch that's important to me. You are." He looked up as the doctor jerked back a curtain and entered.

"How is she?" Travis asked.

"Probably sore as all get-out, unless I miss my guess," the doctor said. "But no broken ribs, so she's free to be released. I don't want her up on horseback for a couple of days, though. The best thing for her, if you can get her to stay still, is bed rest for the next twenty-four hours or so." He shot Rachel a stern look. "Give that black-and-blue body of yours a rest. And don't get your stitches wet."

Rachel made a face. Just the thought of staying in bed for a day made her feel like an invalid. "Can I wash my hair?"

"If you can do it without getting your stitches wet."

"When do the stitches come out?" Rachel asked.

"One week. Think you can handle that?"

"No problem," Travis promised before Rachel could reply. "I'll make sure she gets absolutely everything she needs."

"BUT I DON'T WANT to stay in bed," Rachel argued as Travis drove her home.

"Tough. You heard what the doctor said."

"Can't we at least drive out to the pasture where the stampede occurred?" Rachel persisted.

He slanted her a glance. "You promise me you'll go to bed, as ordered, the moment we get home?"

"Yes."

"You promise me you won't so much as try and get out of the car when we get there, but will be content to

sit and look out the window at your wonderfully behaved cows and repaired fence?''

Rachel was silent a moment. "I don't see what—"

"Now, Miss Rachel," Travis drawled, as if he were
her nanny instead of her friend, "you heard what that
doctor said."

Rachel closed her eyes in defeat. "I promise," she
said.

"You see?" he said once they were there. "Everything's fine."

And it was, Rachel noted with relief. "Rowdy and
the hands did a good job."

"How about you?" Travis asked quietly, his concern etched in the masculine planes of his face. "You
feeling okay?"

Rachel nodded, wanting nothing more at that second than to wrap herself in his strong arms and stay
there for the rest of the day. Not making love necessarily, though that would be very nice, but just being
held. She wanted only to be close to him again, without any complications or outside matters coming in to
separate them.

"I'm fine. Just a little tired, that's all."

When they reached the house, Rachel winced and
unfastened her seat belt. "I don't know how rodeo
cowboys do it," she lamented.

"They've got grit," Travis said, circling around to
help her out of the car. "Just like you do."

"Hey, the boss is back!" Bobby Ray shouted from behind her. Rachel turned to see every hand in the place walking toward her. Tears sprang to her eyes as she saw that Rowdy even had flowers in his hand. He tipped his hat, looking genuinely glad to see her. "Ma'am. We're glad to see you're all right."

"You gave us all a scare," Bobby Ray said. "Not to worry, though. That crazy cow has been sent off to market, just like you asked. And the vet sewed up the calf that got hurt."

"Thank you." Rachel took a deep breath. "I owe you all an apology, though." She visibly searched out each and every hand's eyes. "You told me something like that would happen. It did. I'm sorry I didn't bow to your expertise in the matter. Next time, I promise I will."

"Yeah, well—" Rowdy looked abashed "—we owe you an apology for that jackalope hunt. Guess we're even."

"Oh, come on," Rachel said. "It was funny. Of course," she continued as she ambled slowly and painfully toward the house, "had you sent me on a snipe hunt, I wouldn't have been nearly as gullible, 'cause I know what snipe are."

The men chuckled in unison. "Yeah, well if you want to call a truce and start fresh . . . ?" Rowdy left the thought hanging.

"I'd like that very much," Rachel said graciously. She looked at Rowdy. "I'm going to be laid up for a few days, so if you'll run the ranch in the meantime, I'd appreciate it."

Chapter Fourteen

Travis strode into the ranch-house kitchen and skidded to a stop. His sensual mouth curling upward at the corners, he slouched against the counter and regarded Rachel. "What are you doing out of bed?" he demanded.

"What does it look like I'm doing?" she asked, rolling her eyes. "I'm going to wash my hair."

"Without getting your stitches wet?"

"It won't be easy so I thought I'd ask Jaclyn or Gretchen to help me." She looked around as if noticing for the first time how quiet the house was. A flush of pink crept up her cheeks. "Where are they, anyway?"

"Dinner out and a movie. It's the housekeeper's night off, anyway. I'm in charge of feeding you."

Rachel groaned. "I'm not up to your chili today."

"Nothing that spicy, huh?" Glad to see Rachel was feeling more like her old self after a day in bed, he came closer and grabbed her around the waist.

"Not tonight." She tipped her head back and didn't move away. Travis had the sudden urge to kiss her. Not sure he could stop with just that if he did, he let go of her gently.

"Well, you're in luck if it's bland you want," he said as he looked in the refrigerator. "'Cause what I had in mind was either canned soup or scrambled eggs—"

"I'm not hungry, Travis," she interrupted, the patient in her turning a little temperamental and grumpy. "I just want my hair washed."

He exhaled loudly, then scanned her from the top of her red head to her bare toes. She was wearing a pale pink wraparound robe and a white high-necked nightgown that would have suited a nun. The outfit was so chaste, and yet, on her the overall effect was astonishingly sexy. "One-track mind, huh?" he asked, pretending to be exasperated.

"You can feed me later," Rachel allowed petulantly. "After you've washed my hair."

"Me?" Travis echoed in disbelief.

"You." She gave him a dazzling determined smile, and one hand to his shoulder, propelled him toward the kitchen sink.

"Now wait a minute—"

"I know, I know. You ain't no beauty-parlor operator." Rachel put shampoo bottles on one side of the double sink.

"You're damn right I'm not," Travis grumbled. It was hell to be this close to her, to want her so badly he ached, and not be able to touch her.

Dragging over a chair, she climbed onto the kitchen counter. Using a rolled towel as a neck rest, she prepared to stretch out, so that her hair tumbled into the stainless-steel sink.

"We're going to do this here?"

Rachel's eyes sparkled as she lay down. "Unless you can think of a better place. Would you hand me that plastic wrap please? I want to put it over the bandage."

He complied, then helped her secure it. "I've never done this before."

Her eyes met his. "I have faith in you," she said. "And just think how much better you're going to help me to feel."

Unfortunately that was all Travis could think about. About how it would be to make love to her again. Not in a frenzy of passion this time, of pent-up frustration and desire, but tenderly.

"Unless, of course—" Rachel paused "—you want me to get water in my stitches and risk an infection. Then I suppose I could do it by myself, or at least try."

"That's blackmail," he said gravely.

She lifted a shoulder unapologetically. "Yes, but is it working?"

He only grinned in answer. The thought of sinking his hands into her flame-red tresses wasn't nearly as unpalatable as he pretended. In fact, he noted, suppressing a groan of desire, it was damned sexy, too.

Travis adjusted the water temperature and learned how to work the spray nozzle next to the sink. She talked him through the first rinse, the shampoo, the second rinse, conditioner and third rinse with her eyes closed.

It felt good, having his hands in her hair. Intimate and sensual. And Rachel noted, as she peeked and saw the expression on his face, he didn't seem to be minding the chore all that much. Beyond that, though, it was very hard for her to tell what he was thinking. She knew he desired her, had even come to respect her as a woman and a rancher. But would he ever care enough about her for them to have a real future together? Or was their lovemaking a one-time affair that would never again be repeated?

He squeezed the excess water out of her hair. With his help, they wrapped her hair in a towel and left the plastic wrap where it was, over the bandage.

He held out a hand. "Easy does it," he said as he guided her to a sitting position on the countertop.

Without warning, the room spun as if she were riding a merry-go-round, but Travis's strong arm caught her.

"Dizzy, huh?"

"A little."

"Then that does it."

The next thing Rachel knew she'd been swept up in his arms. His strides long and purposeful, he headed for the stairs.

Rachel's pulse pounded in her ears as he carried her to the second floor. In the dark shirt and jeans, his hair rakishly tousled, the shadow of evening beard on his face, he looked a thousand times more tempting and dangerous and alluring than he ever had.

He placed her gently on the bed, then sank down beside her. Rachel leaned against the pillows. The room had long ago stopped spinning. But she had enjoyed being carted off to bed by him so much she'd been loath to stop it.

"Better?" Travis asked.

Rachel nodded. "Much," she whispered.

He put his hand on top of hers and traced the back of it warmly. "You gave me quite a scare, you know."

"I know." She tried hard not to tremble as he traced yet another evocative pattern on her skin.

He gave her a searching look, this one more fraught with emotion than the last. "I don't ever want to be that scared again," he said.

Rachel's heart soared at the revelation he cared about her deeply and wasn't afraid to show it. "I promise I'll be more careful."

"You damn well better be," he grumbled on a note of genuine relief. "You're important to me, you know. Damn important." His powerful shoulders eclipsed her vision at the same instant his hands framed her face. Rachel had a millisecond to draw a breath, then his mouth came down on hers.

Pleasure sizzled inside her as his tongue swept into her mouth, tasting her until she ached. His hand stroked her body, gentling, arousing. He continued to kiss her until she was drugged with desire, her body rigid and aching with wanting. Rachel wreathed her arms around his neck and held him close. She hadn't realized until just then how much she had yearned for this. She clung to him wholeheartedly, surrendering to the steamy sensuality of his embrace and yet demanding of it at the same time. She couldn't taste him deeply enough. Couldn't feel him close enough. Couldn't get enough.

And even though nothing like this had ever happened to her before, she knew it was dangerous for her to let herself feel this way. Dangerous to let it continue the way he obviously wanted it to continue. "Travis," she moaned, moving her mouth from his, "this isn't fair." He still didn't want marriage.

"I know all the reasons why not, Rachel," he said, his breath coming as fast and hard as hers. His eyes scanned her face tenderly. "I've gone over them myself a million times. But it always comes back to this. You've got something no other woman has ever had for me, something I can't turn away from," he admitted gruffly. "And judging from the way you kiss me, I think I have a hell of a lot to offer you, too."

Then his mouth was on hers again. And there was no more time to think, only to feel. And feel she did. Her senses were inundated with the touch and taste of him. He was so hard and strong. He smelled so good, so evocatively male. And damn him, he knew just how to kiss her. Just how to wring a response from her. Not that she seemed to be fighting it all that much, she realized, dazed. Their innate differences aside, she knew Travis was right. What they were experiencing was something special. Certainly no one had ever made her feel like this. So soft and feminine and helplessly wanton. No other man had ever made her feel the urgent need to be one with him.

He tilted his head and kissed her from another angle. When he lifted his head again, he stroked his hand down her neck into the open collar of her nightgown.

"Oh, Travis," Rachel murmured, as the last of her resistance crumbled and heat tunneled through her in wave after delicious wave.

He paused. "I love you, Rachel. Before this goes any further, I want you to know that." He looked into her eyes and her heart soared.

"Oh, Travis. I love you, too," she said, her lip trembling with the emotional price of the admission.

"Oh, yeah?"

"Oh, yeah," she murmured sexily, just holding him close for a moment.

"Well, that's good 'cause you're everything I've ever wanted in a woman. Everything. I realized that

yesterday when I saw you get dragged off that horse."
He buried his face in the fragrant dampness of her
hair. "I don't know what I'd ever do without you,
Rachel," he confessed, his voice lowering another
thoroughly possessive notch. "God knows I sure don't
want to find out."

Rachel drew back so she could see the rugged lines
of his face. "Staking a claim, cowboy?"

He grinned back at her. "You bet." Deliberately he
threaded his fingers through her hair and put pressure at her nape to draw her head up and back, until
it was precisely under his. "In the best way I know
how," he finished softly. His face as he looked at her,
all warm and tender and loving, made her want to cry.

"Oh, Travis," Rachel whispered.

"That's right," he whispered back. "Say my name.
Say it over and over and over again."

Nothing had ever felt as good or as right as the
touch of his lips on hers. The rest of the world blurred.
Again they kissed, until there was only this moment,
only the two of them alone, and the love they had
professed for one another.

He shifted his hands to her hips and pulled her
against him. She welcomed the thrusting pressure just
as she welcomed his tongue in her mouth and minutes
later, when the kiss finally ended, the feel of his palm
warmly caressing the slope of her neck. She could tell
by the look in his eyes that this time he wasn't going

to stop, not unless she made him. And she knew she wasn't going to make him.

This time... this once, she was simply going to enjoy what life had given her, take all the pleasure and forget the problems that undoubtedly lay ahead.

He bent to kiss her again, deeply and thoroughly. She reached out blindly for him, seeking his love and the tenderness she knew he had to give.

Breathing raggedly, he drew away and rested his forehead against hers. His heart was thundering in his chest, just as hers was. "No regrets this time, Rachel," he vowed.

"No regrets," she promised.

His eyes darkened. "You're sure?" he teased. "You're not delirious with pain, are you?"

Wordlessly she undid the snaps on his shirt and slipped her hand inside. "Make love to me, Travis," Rachel whispered, caressing the solidness of his chest and guiding him close. "Make love to me now."

Groaning, he stretched out beside her. They undressed one another slowly, provocatively.

"You're beautiful."

"So are you."

"I never thought this would happen." Rachel breathed in sharply as he touched her.

He grinned. "I did."

They laughed together, softly, wantonly.

If this wasn't heaven, Rachel thought, it was as close as it got. She closed her eyes, loving the feel of the sandpapery stubble on his face as it brushed against the softness of her breasts. His mouth, hot and rapacious, wetly covered her nipples and urged them to life.

An aching sizzled through her, from breasts to stomach to thighs. "Oh, Travis, I want you," she murmured. Her thighs turned to liquid and fell open even farther, and her hips tilted up and forward.

He let his eyes roam her body. "Then show me."

She touched him. "Like this?"

He moaned and caught her hand. "Yes, like this," he said.

He rolled toward her. For long moments they lay side by side in the pale moonlight washing in through the windows, reveling in the glorious difference of her pliant curves and his silky hardness. They stroked and explored. Their glances met. His eyes filled with love. "Let's do everything, Travis," she persuaded softly, her hand closing around his warm male heat. "Absolutely everything."

And they did.

Kissing without touching. Touching without kissing. Touching and kissing simultaneously. Rachel climaxed once, twice, until at last, impatient, he eased the weight and length of his body over hers. His eyes were both serious and tender as he moved against her, then inside her with excruciating care.

Her senses reeled with pleasure as he began to move, at first with sensual deliberation, then more and more passionately until she was rocking beneath him, aware only of the heat and the building pressure, the mindless urgent need for release.

She felt it all, reveled in it. And still he couldn't, wouldn't, stop, not until they had both given of themselves as never before, until they were both ravished, fulfilled and utterly exhausted.

The quiet that followed the crescendo of their love-making was riveting. And anything but relaxing.

Rachel moved slightly so her head was no longer on his chest. She was glad it was dark now. Glad they were alone. Moments ago, embroiled in the heat of their passion, of her urgent need to be with him, of the wonder of their mutually professed love, she'd felt freer than she had in years. Now, with the rush of pleasure fading, she only felt afraid. She didn't want anything to spoil their newfound happiness, and she was desperately afraid something would.

The ringing phone broke the silence.

His arm still around her, Travis reached for the receiver beside the bed. "Hang on a minute, Rowdy," he said, after he'd listened for a moment. "I'll get her."

Rachel flushed guiltily, as she thought about what had happened. She'd done what she'd sworn she would never do. She had become a cowboy's mistress.

Wasn't it ironic, she thought, that Travis looked completely at ease about the compromising nature of their intense attraction and love for one another, while she was now a bundle of conflicted feelings? She wanted to be with Travis. She wanted to make love with him, and be loved by him. And yet she didn't want anyone to know about it, for fear it would undermine her authority. But that wasn't Travis's fault. All he'd ever professed to want was to make wild passionate love to her. She sent Travis a smile as she accepted the phone.

"Hi, Rowdy. What's up?" She listened a moment. "Good. No. Nothing further. All right. I'll see you first thing tomorrow. Thanks."

She handed the phone back to Travis. While he hung up the receiver, she scooted off the bed.

"What'd Rowdy want?"

"Just to tell me how things are going." Needing suddenly to get out of the house, to have time to think, she started for her bureau.

Travis lay back against the pillows, his hands folded behind his head. "Now what are you doing?" he asked.

"Dressing. I'm going down to the stables to check out that calf that got hurt yesterday."

Travis sat up halfway and propped his weight on his elbow. "Why, if he's fine?"

Rachel pulled a shirt from the closet and a handful of undies from her bureau. "I just want to see him myself."

"I thought the doctor told you to stay in bed," Travis pointed out. His eyes sparkled suggestively as he patted the place beside him.

"He told me to stay in bed and rest," Rachel corrected. She grinned at Travis as he continued to try to coax her back into bed. "I wasn't resting."

His look immediately turned to one of concern. He caught her hand as she passed him and drew her down, so that she was seated on the edge of the bed. Lifting her hand to his mouth, he gently kissed her fingertips. "I didn't hurt you, did I?"

He looked deep into her eyes, and for a moment it was all Rachel could do not to get lost in the slate-blue depths. "No," she said softly, remembering all too well how wonderful he had been to her. "You made me feel better than I have in a long time, Travis." *More a woman. More loved.*

"Then why the rush to leave?" he asked softly, trailing a hand down her spine.

Was this what it would be like from now on? Rachel wondered, as she tried with all her might to resist him. Would Travis be constantly trying to lure her into bed? Would she be torn between her duty and her desires?

"Why not let the calf wait until tomorrow?"

"Because I have a responsibility," Rachel returned abruptly, irritated she should have to spell this out to Travis when he knew darn well the depth of her commitment to the ranch and to every living thing on it.

And she felt most irritated because they would have to be careful to hide their affair. How could she even think of doing that around her children?

Travis's grip on her waist gentled from a persuasive touch to a soft sultry stroking caress that made her insides go to mush. The look he gave her was hot and steamy. She felt the by now familiar languidness between her thighs and just as determinedly ignored her sensual reaction to his nearness. She told herself it didn't matter. She had a business to run.

"Want me to go with you?" He watched as she modestly draped the top sheet around her middle and scooped up a handful of her clothes. He leapt agilely to his feet, then followed her into her adjacent private bathroom.

Rachel glanced yearningly at the huge marble tub, then thought no. Odds were, if she stepped into that even for a second, Travis would follow.

Determinedly she reached for a washcloth and held it under warm running water. She would've preferred to shut the door, but with him standing gloriously naked against the jamb, there wasn't a lot she could do.

"Look, I'll go down to the barn for you, if you want. You don't have to go down there tonight," Travis said.

"Thanks." Rachel cut him off brusquely. "But I want to go."

Rachel knew her motivation for going out went much deeper. The truth, whether she wanted to admit it to Travis or not, was that she still hadn't found a buyer for the organically raised herd, and she was beginning to feel panicky. The only time she could really relax was when she was actively working toward her goals and tending to the ranch. And right now, she didn't want to think about failing—or how complicated her personal life had just become.

Rachel shrugged. "I just think I'll sleep better after I've seen him again."

"Once a softy, always a softy," he teased. "Miss Rachel, you are all heart."

"You make me feel that way," she confessed.

"That's always been my intent."

They exchanged smiles. Glancing up, she caught a glimpse of herself in the mirror and was amazed at how loved she looked. How different, with her mouth all red and swollen and thoroughly kissed. Her cheeks were flushed, and above the tightly wrapped sheet, the uppermost curves of her breasts were pink and tender and tingling.

And right behind her, Travis stood proudly, watching her, as bold as she was shy. And why not? she asked herself on a reluctant sigh as she ran a brush through the damp ends of her hair. He had every right to be proud of his physique. His body was tanned and fit and lightly covered with whorls of dark hair. Lower still was the velvety sight of his burgeoning arousal. Just looking at him made Rachel draw in her breath sharply.

"Here," he said gently, untucking the corners of the sheet where it was snuggled between her breasts. He reached for the warm wet washcloth. "Let me."

Rachel caught the sheet a half second before it fell completely. Deliberately she avoided his eyes. She knew if she looked at him directly, if she kissed him just once, she would be lost. Gloriously lost. "No, Travis. Don't."

"Why not?" he said softly as his playful mood faded.

"Because even though I love you, I've got to pull myself together and get back to managing the ranch."

"Do you?" he asked. When she didn't answer, he rubbed his hands over her bare arms and confessed gently, "Rowdy let me look at the books, Rachel." She tried to turn away, but he held her firmly in place. His voice was gentle but stern. "I know you're still in trouble. But don't you see? It doesn't matter anymore, now that we've got each other."

Rachel stared up at him in disbelief. "It matters terribly, Travis!" she disagreed, more sharply than she had intended. "I can't let your mother and the twins down." And she had so little time left to secure her children's inheritance.

"You haven't let anyone down," Travis argued kindly.

"Haven't I?" Rachel sighed. "I've taken a ranch that was operating in the black and turned it into one that is operating in the red. What do you call that?"

Travis's lips compressed grimly. "No one on this ranch doubts how hard you've tried."

He was speaking as if the gig were up. Rachel's shoulders stiffened defensively. "It's not over yet, Travis," she warned.

"Not even if I want it to be?" Travis challenged, his eyes dark, his voice edged with tension.

Rachel sensed a gauntlet had been thrown down between them. Her heart started pounding.

"I love you, Rachel," Travis whispered, drawing her into his arms and holding her close. His breath whispered across the shampooed freshness of her hair. "I love you with all my heart." He squeezed her tightly. "Regardless of what happens with the ranch, I'll never stop."

"Oh, Travis," Rachel whispered, holding him close. She rested her face against his shoulder. "I love you, too. I really do."

"Then marry me," Travis said passionately. He hooked his finger beneath her chin and lifted her face to his.

And suddenly, for Rachel, it was as if history was repeating itself. She spun away from Travis, aware she had never felt more miserable in her life. "I can't," she said. But wasn't this what she had wanted?

If he was stung by her rejection, he didn't show it. "Why not? You'll still have the ranch."

"But it'll be for all the wrong reasons!" she cried.

He stared at her incredulously. "Because you love me and agreed to be my wife?"

"Because I won't have *earned* it," she explained.

"Oh, I don't know about that," he teased, his wicked grin colored with relief. He pulled her to him and held her against the strong hard length of him. "Being married to me could be hell."

She laughed softly at the exaggeration in his words. "Knowing what a Texas bad boy you are, Travis Westcott, truer words were never spoken." She looked up at him, all the love she felt for him in her eyes. "But I still can't marry you," she said, sticking to her guns. "At least not now. Not yet." *Not until I've accomplished what I set out to do.*

"Because of the ranch?" The tenseness came back into his face.

"I'm not going to marry into it, not this time," Rachel countered intractably.

"Then don't." Travis shrugged. "Go back to work as a travel agent. If you want, you could even start your own agency here in San Angelo. It won't matter what you do. We'll be together."

"I want to ranch," Rachel insisted stubbornly.

"Then do that," he advised, exasperated. "As my wife."

"No."

His jaw set, he stared at her and shook his head. Rachel could tell he was about to lose his temper. "This is stupid. You love me. I love you."

"I'm not discounting any of that," she whispered miserably.

"Then what are you trying to tell me?"

She faced him boldly. "That it's not over yet. That I still have two weeks to make good on my deal with your mother and earn this ranch for the twins."

"Face it, Rachel," he said, making no effort to temper his words this time. "You are never going to sell that herd, at least not at the kind of price that you want and need."

"You don't know that!"

"The hell I don't! I've been in this business a darn sight longer than you have."

"In a peripheral sense, maybe."

His jaw tautened. "And if you don't sell that herd, you'll never get back in the black in time to earn the right to run this ranch."

Rachel flung her washcloth back into the sink and rushed past him. "That's a fine thing to say to me, Travis!"

He stomped after her and yanked on his jeans. "Oh. Now I get it. Now you're saying you want me to lie to spare your feelings. Well, I won't do that!"

Rachel picked up his shirt and his boots and flung them at him. "I should've known you wouldn't believe in me."

Travis ducked as one of his socks came flying past his head. "I never said that." He yanked on his shirt and fastened the pearl snaps. He was halfway done when he realized he'd put the two edges of the shirt together crookedly. Muttering curses through his teeth, he ripped open the snaps and started again. "I just said there's nothing more you can do that you haven't already done."

"Yes, there is," Rachel said as she pulled on her own jeans and boots.

"Yeah?" Travis sat down on the side of the bed and yanked on his boots. "Like what?"

"I'm going to hire a photographer and a publicist!" she announced haughtily.

He gave her a funny look. "To do what?"

"To help me put together a brochure and maybe even a video to help sell my Brahmas. Only this time, instead of trying to sell the merits of those calves I bought, I'm going to sell the whole ranch, instead. I'm going to sell the Westcott reputation for excellence."

Travis's glance narrowed. He stood slowly. "What if it doesn't work?"

His continued lack of faith in her stung. "It will." Fully dressed, she breezed past him.

He followed her out the door and down the stairs. "But what if it doesn't?"

She swallowed hard and held back the hot bitter tears of defeat. "Then I go home to Beaumont," she said thickly. "The twins can start school there in the fall."

Travis sighed. Was he going to have to buy a herd of his own cows in order to keep her? He stepped lithely in front of her, blocking her way. "And we're over?" He snapped his fingers. "Just like that?"

Rachel swallowed. She backed up until her spine grazed a wall. "I didn't say that." Her head lifted proudly as her heart did battle with her pride. "Of course I'd still see you, if...if you want," she finished uncertainly.

Hurt glimmered in Travis's eyes. "As what?" he commanded hoarsely. "My mistress?"

"Your lover," Rachel corrected. "And that isn't such a bad thing," she said persuasively. "You said so yourself. We'd be partners, equal in all respects..."

Travis's breath blew out slowly. "I don't want a lover anymore, someone I see only on occasion, Rachel. I want a wife. A family. And I want to live on this ranch."

He was offering her everything she had ever wanted. Yet she knew from bitter experience how such a marriage would be received by the community at large. Her motivations would be suspect, and she couldn't go through that again. She couldn't put her children through it, either. Earning her own way was laudable. Sponging off someone else was not. She would not be thought a gold digger. Never again. "I can't do that, Travis," she said quietly.

They stared at one another in heated silence for a moment. "Is this ranch really more important to you than I am?"

"Travis—"

"That's the bottom line, isn't it?" He slammed both his palms against the wall. "Your career—your ultimate goals—come first."

"You're being unreasonable," she asserted angrily. She had expected him to understand her. It infuriated her that he didn't. Using her elbow to push him aside, she stomped off toward the kitchen.

"I'm being unreasonable?" Travis stormed after her.

"If the situation was reversed, I'd give you a chance to work things out career-wise."

"I'm giving you the chance," Travis said, his voice vibrating with tension. His eyes bored into hers. "I just want you to do it as my wife!"

"Why can't we just be lovers now?" she pleaded softly. After all, he was the one who had suggested it.

Travis took her in his arms and held her. "Because I love you and I want to be with you." He stroked her hair with his hand. "And we have to set a good example for your kids."

"Now you're talking like a father!" She had never felt more miserable and misunderstood and maligned than she did at that moment. Worse, once again, the Westcott ranch was standing between her and Travis.

"You're telling me you'd be comfortable to continue on as we are, with the two of us having to sneak around? That's why you're going out, isn't it? To make sure you won't get caught in a compromising position when my mom and the kids get back."

Rachel flushed guiltily and wished fervently everything wasn't so confused. "That's part of it," she admitted slowly.

"So how would we see each other? Would I pay my mom a quarter to take the kids somewhere? Would we rendezvous in the attic at high noon or just meet outside at midnight, and pray none of the hands happen to come along and see us?"

"You're not only being ridiculous, you're being crude," Rachel countered.

"Practical," he corrected sternly, still keeping her in his arms. "And it's about time one of us was."

"I need time, Travis."

He studied her sadly. "And I'm telling you, time has run out. We've wasted half our lives, Rachel. Is it so wrong of me not to want to waste another minute and to want to sleep with you in my arms every night? Is it so wrong of me to want to tell the whole world I love you?"

No, it wasn't wrong. It was what she had once longed to hear more than anything in the world. Unfortunately the timing just wasn't right. "I can't marry you when I'm a failure," she said. "Please try and understand."

"What the hell do you think I've been trying to do?" he said. He released her and moved past her.

"Travis—"

He grabbed his hat off the hook next to the door, slapped it on his head and stalked to the door. "Let me know if you change your mind." He went out and the screen door slammed behind him. "If you ever do!" he shouted after a moment. "Until then, I'll be in Fort Worth!"

Chapter Fifteen

"Good news?" Jaclyn asked, as she entered the ranch-house office carrying a silver tea service on a tray.

Rachel nodded. "The best. I found a buyer for my herd. They'll be giving me a down payment when they sign the contract later today, and that money will put the ranch back in the black. Plus, they're interested in a long-term arrangement. I haven't worked out the terms with them yet, but I'm confident we can arrange something."

"I'm impressed. The brochures you had printed really worked," Jaclyn said.

Rachel nodded, satisfied. "I think the video helped, too. The combination of the two was a very effective marketing tool."

"So why don't you look happier?" Jaclyn asked. She poured them both a cup of tea. She paused. Her expression grew troubled. "It's Travis, isn't it?"

"Yes," Rachel admitted on a tremulous sigh. She hadn't seen him in two weeks.

The corners of Jaclyn's mouth edged upward into a reflective smile. "I thought so."

Rachel studied her mother-in-law, wondering if she was up to hearing the truth. "You may as well know. I'm in love with him," she blurted out.

Jaclyn smiled and sat in a chair opposite Rachel. "I figured that, too."

"You're not upset?"

"Honey, I love you." Jaclyn got up, walked around the desk and hugged her warmly. "Why would I be upset?"

"Because I drove him away."

"No," Jaclyn corrected, giving Rachel another quick spirit-bolstering hug before resuming her seat, "you brought him home."

"For the summer, maybe," Rachel allowed.

"For good," Jaclyn interrupted. "His heart is here now, on the ranch. Travis never would've realized how much his heritage really meant to him, or understood the importance of passing our heritage on to the next generation of Westcotts if you hadn't understood it yourself and been here to show him, Rachel."

Jaclyn's admiration made Rachel feel she had accomplished something important. "I thought earning the right to run the ranch would make me happy," Rachel said slowly. "I thought living here would give me the respectability and sense of family and belonging I've always craved."

Jaclyn studied her, a compassionate look in her blue eyes. "And it hasn't?"

Rachel shrugged. "I thought I'd be delirious with my success. But..."

"You're not."

"No. I just feel empty." She held up both hands before Jaclyn could interrupt. "Don't get me wrong. I'm proud of myself, but I thought it would mean more. I thought running the ranch was all it would take to make me happy."

"And it's not?"

"No," Rachel admitted. Tears shimmered in her eyes. "I miss your son desperately."

"Have you told him?"

Rachel let out a shaky laugh and wiped at her eyes. "No."

"Why not?"

"He was so furious with me when we last talked, before he left." And with good reason, Rachel acknowledged silently. He'd said he loved her! He'd actually asked her to marry him! And what had she done? She'd said no. And why? Because she had let her pride get in the way. She saw now how wrong she'd been to put the ranch ahead of everything, including the man she loved.

"My mother had a saying. There's never anything that can't be fixed. If you try hard enough, that is." Jaclyn looked at Rachel long and hard. "Are you willing to try hard enough?"

Rachel knew, given half a chance, she and Travis could be happy together. Happier than either of them had ever dreamed. "You really think Travis will forgive me?"

Jaclyn smiled. "No one ever went wrong following their heart."

TRAVIS WAS in his Fort Worth office. He stood as she entered, his expression one of concern and caution. "Is everything all right at the ranch?"

"Yes." *And no,* she thought, *not without you.*

Her heart pounding, she gestured at a chair in the luxuriously appointed office. It was quite different from the cramped sewing room he had been using. "May I sit down and speak with you a moment?"

"I've always got time for you," he said, his face inscrutable, his eyes intense. "You know that."

Rachel sat down gratefully and clasped her hands in front of her, willing them to stop trembling. "Now that I'm here, I've got so much to say I don't know where to start." *Or even if you are going to want to hear it.*

His eyes held hers. He looked tired, she thought, as if he hadn't been sleeping well, either.

"Take your time."

She tore her eyes from his. "About the ranch."

"I heard about your success with the organically raised herd," he said before she could continue.

"Rowdy and my mother both phoned to tell me. Congratulations."

"Thanks," she said awkwardly.

"I didn't think you could do it." He smiled at her and his voice dropped a compelling notch. "You proved me wrong."

She hadn't expected him to be happy for her or look so proud of her success. It made her feel even worse about the way she'd turned her back on him. As if she'd betrayed him.

"About the ranch and the deal I made with your mother..." she began. His mouth tightened unhappily at the mention of the Bar W, and seeing his defenses rise, she had to force herself to go on. "Your mother gave me papers making me conservator of the ranch for the children, but I can't sign them. I've thought about it, and I know now it wouldn't be right."

He studied her tensely, looking no happier than he had before she'd told him she was giving it all up. "You're telling me you're leaving? Now?"

Please, don't let it be too late. "No. At least I don't want to," she replied. Her heart was in her throat. Her eyes locked with his. She took a deep bolstering breath, trying not to let her emotions overcome her. "I'd like to stay on, either in the same capacity as ranch manager, answerable to you and Jaclyn, or as a hired hand, or an assistant to Rowdy."

"Whoa!" Looking as somber and uncertain as she felt, Travis put up an imperious hand to stop her and circled around to the front of his desk. "What brought this on?"

It's now or never. Lose my pride or the man I love forever. "My love for you," she said simply. Mouth trembling, she got to her feet and took his hands in hers. She squeezed them tightly, taking her strength from his. Her mouth trembled as she tilted her head back and looked deep into his eyes. "I realized I was a fool to turn down your offer of marriage. And I'm so very sorry I hurt you. Oh Travis," she whispered. "I do love you."

"I love you, too," he said. He wrapped his arms about her waist and brought her against him. She snuggled against his warmth, aware that nothing had ever felt so right as the two of them together. And nothing ever would.

"Can you forgive me for being so foolish?" she asked.

He kissed her deeply, thoroughly, and with a dangerous lack of restraint. "Of course I can forgive you."

"But—"

"That's over now, Rachel." He squeezed her tightly, so that they were touching everywhere. "We don't have to talk of it again."

Hope for the future flared in her heart, and Rachel found she suddenly had more courage than she knew. "Does that mean you still want to marry me?"

He bent his head and answered her with a slow searing kiss that curled her toes and weakened her knees. When they were both breathless and aching, he lifted his head. "If you'll have me, hell yes, the offer still stands," he said gruffly. "In fact," he said, further delineating his plans, "I want to marry you as soon as possible."

"Oh, Travis," Rachel cried, joy exploding inside her like fireworks in a Texas sky, "I want that, too."

His hand stroked her hair lovingly, drifted lower, down her back. "And if you'd waited one more day until I cleared my desk of everything urgent, I would've come out to the ranch myself and asked you again," Travis said, squeezing her waist. "In the meantime—" one arm still around her shoulders, he reached behind him for a manila folder with her name on it "—I have an early wedding present for you."

She sent him a puzzled look and then opened it, gasping at what she saw. "Travis!"

"Those are papers stating that I give up all present and future claims to the ranch, whether you marry me or not. I was going to give you those and then propose all over again."

She couldn't help it, she started to laugh. He stared bemusedly into her flushed face. "Is the idea of marrying me that hilarious?"

"No. It's just that I'm trying to give up the ranch. And you're trying to give it to me." She shook her head in rueful contemplation.

"And we both want to get married," he finished, a satisfied gleam in his eyes.

"Yes." She sobered briefly. "I do want that," she whispered, "very much."

"Then there's only one solution." Travis sat down in a chair and pulled her onto his lap. "We'll just have to co-own the ranch."

"You won't mind doing that?"

He shook his head. "I no longer need the Bar W." He anchored both arms around her and held her close. "And I don't want anything that keeps me away from you. I love you, Rachel." He touched a hand to the side of her face. "And that's all that counts." Hands at her nape, he brought her head down to his.

When at last they drew apart, she sighed in contentment, the glow of his love for her and hers for him filling her with renewed warmth. "Well, what do you think?" she teased softly. "Shall we find someplace nice and quiet?"

"I have a condo close by."

The prospect of making love with him again filled her with heat and longing. "So what are we waiting for, cowboy?"

He grinned, his eyes twinkling merrily. "Not a damn thing."

ABOUT THE AUTHOR
Cathy Gillen Thacker is a full-time novelist who once taught piano to
children. Born and raised in Ohio, she attended Miami University. After
moving cross-country several times, she settled in Texas with her
husband and three children. *The Cowboy's Mistress* is Cathy's thirtieth
novel.

Books by Cathy Gillen Thacker
HARLEQUIN AMERICAN ROMANCE
367—IT'S ONLY TEMPORARY
388—FATHER OF THE BRIDE
407—AN UNEXPECTED FAMILY
423—TANGLED WEB
445—HOME FREE
452—ANYTHING'S POSSIBLE

HARLEQUIN INTRIGUE
104—DREAM SPINNERS
137—SLALOM TO TERROR

Don't miss any of our special offers. Write to us at the following address
for information on our newest releases.

Harlequin Reader Service
P.O. Box 1397, Buffalo, NY 14240
Canadian address: P.O. Box 603,
Fort Erie, Ont. L2A 5X3

CGTB10

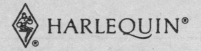 HARLEQUIN®

THE TAGGARTS OF TEXAS!

Harlequin's Ruth Jean Dale brings you
THE TAGGARTS OF TEXAS!

Those Taggart men—strong, sexy and hard to resist...

You've met Jesse James Taggart in FIREWORKS!
Harlequin Romance #3205 (July 1992)

Now meet Trey Smith—he's THE RED-BLOODED YANKEE!
Harlequin Temptation #413 (October 1992)

Then there's Daniel Boone Taggart in SHOWDOWN!
Harlequin Romance #3242 (January 1993)

And finally the Taggarts who started it all—in LEGEND!
Harlequin Historical #168 (April 1993)

Read all the Taggart romances!
Meet all the Taggart men!

Available wherever Harlequin books are sold.

A SPAULDING AND DARIEN MYSTERY

Amateur sleuths Jenny Spaulding and Peter Darien have set the date for their wedding. But before they walk down the aisle, love must pass a final test. This time, they won't have to solve a murder, they'll have to prevent one—Jenny's. Don't miss the chilling conclusion to the SPAULDING AND DARIEN MYSTERY series in October. Watch for:

#197 WHEN SHE WAS BAD by Robin Francis

Look for the identifying series flash—A SPAULDING AND DARIEN MYSTERY—and join Jenny and Peter for danger and romance. . . .

HARLEQUIN
AMERICAN · ROMANCE®

American Romance's yearlong celebration continues.... Join your favorite authors as they celebrate love set against the special times each month throughout 1992.

Next month... Spooky things were expected in Salem, Massachusetts, on Halloween. But when a tall, dark and gorgeous man emerged from the mist, Holly Bennett thought that was going too far. Was he a real man... or a warlock? Find out in:

OCTOBER

S	M	T	W	T	F	S
					2	3
4					9	10
11	12		15	16	17
18	19			23	24
25	26	27	28	29	30	31

#457
UNDER HIS SPELL
by Linda Randall Wisdom

Read all the *Calendar of Romance* titles, coming to you one per month, all year, only in American Romance.

If you missed any of the *Calendar of Romance* titles—#421 *Happy New Year, Darling;* #425 *Valentine Hearts and Flowers;* #429 *Flannery's Rainbow;* #433 *A Man for Easter;* #437 *Cinderella Mom;* #441 *Daddy's Girl;* #445 *Home Free;* #449 *Opposing Camps;* or #455 *Sand Man*—and would like to order them, send your name, address, zip or postal code, along with a check or money order for $3.29 each for #421 and #425 or $3.39 each for #429, #433, #437, #441, #445, #449, or #455, plus 75¢ postage and handling ($1.00 in Canada) *for each book ordered,* payable to Harlequin Reader Service to:

In the U.S.	In Canada
3010 Walden Avenue	P.O. Box 609
P.O. Box 1325	Fort Erie, Ontario
Buffalo, NY 14269-1325	L2A 5X3

Please specify book title(s) with your order.
Canadian residents add applicable federal and provincial taxes.

COR10